# Guns & Glitter

Cameron Hart

Published by Cameron Hart, 2024.

GUNS & GLITTER

**First edition. February 23, 2024.**



ISBN: 979-8224810215

Written by Cameron Hart.

# Want a free book?

**Sign up for my newsletter**[1] and get your free copy of Chasing Stacy!

One look at the stunning waitress carrying the weight of the world on her shoulders, and I'm a goner. I wasn't looking for a sweet little thing with auburn hair and more baggage than I can fit on the back of my bike, but there's no going back now. She's mine. I'll prove to her I'm more than capable of handling her past and making her feel safe again.

---

1. https://dl.bookfunnel.com/7wbqvhsx8r

# Connect with me!

Check out my website, cameronhart.net[2], for sneak previews on my latest projects.

## Follow me on social media:

**Facebook Page** - facebook.com/cameronhartauthor
**Instagram** - instagram.com/cameron.hart.author
**TikTok** - tiktok.com/@author.cameron.hart
**Goodreads** - goodreads.com/16081533.Cameron_Hart
**Bookbub** - bookbub.com/authors/cameron-hart

2. https://cameronhart.net/

# Chapter 1

*Logan*

I pour another shot of whiskey because why the fuck not? I finally have a Saturday evening all to myself with no one and nothing to bother me. Just the way I like it.

I left the excitement behind me when I got out of the Marines. Six tours overseas were more than enough action for one lifetime. Now I get my kicks running my own security company with my two best friends, Colton and Slater.

Watchdog Protection, Inc. is a small operation with just the three of us as full-time employees. We're all ex-Marines and served together at one point or another. I was the first to get out, followed by Colton, the burly cowboy with an easy smile and enough charm to fill his home state of Texas. The cocky son-of-a-bitch knows it, too, but he's still one of the best men I know.

When Slater was honorably discharged after landing on a roadside bomb and fucking up his leg and shoulder, he was in bad shape, and not just physically. I'm not sure what all went down while he was overseas on that last tour, but the nearly seven-foot giant was in a lot of pain and darkness for a long time.

Colton and I stuck by him, even moved in briefly when Slater was released from the hospital, despite his many protests. He's still haunted by his demons, though having Watchdog has helped all of us settle and adjust to life as civilians.

It was my idea to use our training and skills to open up our own security firm. Colton was like an excited dog with a bone when I brought it up to him, while Slater objected and tried convincing me he was no good for stuff like that anymore.

Yeah, Colton and I didn't let him get away with that shit. Fast forward several years, and here we are, successful business owners and bachelors to boot. We want for nothing and we rely on no one but ourselves.

Propping my feet up on my coffee table, I lean back on my couch, tipping my head up and taking a deep breath.

Solitude.

Silence.

It might not be much to some people, but to me, it's everything. My life has been nothing but chaos from the moment I was born. Took me damn near forty years to find a little peace, and I plan to enjoy every fucking minute.

I'm about to throw back the second shot of whiskey when my phone rings.

"Son of a bitch," I mutter, setting the glass down.

Staring at the screen, I debate whether I want to answer it or not. I don't recognize the number, but that doesn't mean much. The only numbers saved on my phone are Colton's, Slater's, and the landline for Watchdog. Oh, and the pizza joint down the road.

As much as I want to let the call go to voicemail, I know I need to answer it. Being in the protection business means I'm on call twenty-four seven. Colton just got back from an assignment early this morning and Slater is going to start a job at the library of all places soon, so I'm up if we get a new client. So much for a night off.

Sighing heavily, I wipe a hand down my face, tugging at my scruffy beard.

"Watchdog Protection," I answer the phone, my voice more than a little gruff.

"Logan? Is that you?"

It takes me a second to place the voice. "Marcus? Shit, what's it been? Ten years?"

"Closer to twenty, old friend," he chuckles.

"Marcus Collins," I say more to myself than to him.

We did basic training together; I was just eighteen and he was twenty-one at the time. We struggled through the brutal training required of all soldiers and were put in the same unit until he was reassigned.

I went off on my first tour with Colton and Slater and we lost touch, but the bond we formed during those first few years was solid, apparently even to this day.

"Logan Bennett," he says, jarring me out of my memories. "I wish I had time to catch up, and I really wish this call were under better circumstances," Marcus starts.

"What's going on? How can I help?" You better believe I'd still lay my life down for any of the men and women I served with, no matter how brief the time.

"Well, I heard you were running a security company these days. Protection for hire and whatnot. Is that true?"

"I think if you were able to find my cell phone number, you also had access to my work history," I reply, a smirk on my face.

"Guilty as charged," he admits, though there's no remorse in his voice. "But I needed someone I can trust with my daughter."

I stand up from my couch and go to the kitchen, rummaging around in the drawers until I find a notepad and pen. I always think better if I have a list of actionable items in front of me.

Tossing the paper and pen on the kitchen counter, I begin pacing back and forth, waiting for my old friend to tell me more.

"She has a stalker and the police—"

"Can't do anything until there's proof," I finish for him.

"Well, yes, that, but also...this is a rather sensitive case," Marcus hedges.

"Start at the beginning," I tell him as I grab the pen and remove the cap, poised to write everything down.

Marcus tells me that he and his daughter live in San Francisco, then goes on to relay what little he knows about the stalker. I ask him more about his daughter, making a note that she's twenty, her name is Spencer, she doesn't have many friends, and she still lives at home.

"Is Spencer's mother in the picture?"

There's silence on the other end of the line, then a quiet, "She's no longer with us."

I make note of that as well, though I don't press the issue. I know nothing about relationships and even less about marriage. I couldn't possibly begin to understand what it means to love someone, let alone what it would feel like to lose them.

"How long will you need my services?" I continue. I don't know how to deal with messy emotions, but I can plan, organize, and execute missions to perfection, so that's what I'm focusing on.

"I'm actually leaving the country tomorrow for two weeks. I have a business deal in Paris I need to close."

I'm a little shocked that he's leaving the country if he feels his daughter is in danger, but what do I know about having a family?

"Sounds important," I say, instead of questioning his decision. "What is it you do nowadays? You already know my job."

"Mergers and acquisitions."

"Sounds thrilling," I say dryly.

Marcus laughs. "It keeps me busy and it pays the bills."

I wait for him to continue, but he doesn't. I make another note about Marcus's vague job description and his need to leave the country. I also put an asterisk next to the words *sensitive case*. I know what he means without him having to say it. No police involvement.

That would normally put me on edge, but this is Marcus. I trust him. Still, all of these details help. It could be someone from his place of work or a client he screwed over. All avenues I'll need to research as soon as I end this call.

"Listen, Logan," he says, clearing his throat. "I haven't been...I haven't always been a good father. I didn't know what to do with my little girl after her mom...goddamnit," he mutters.

"I'll take care of your daughter, Marcus. I'll keep her safe."

He blows out a breath and I can almost see him nodding and tapping his left foot on the ground, just like he used to do in basic. "Thank you. I'll pay double your normal rate since this is last minute and requires travel."

"No fucking way," I argue.

"Logan…"

"I won't take money from you."

"We'll talk about it later. Right now, book a flight to sunny San Francisco."

I grunt and we say our goodbyes.

Looking over at the unfinished shot of whiskey on the coffee table, I shake my head. Twenty minutes ago I was looking forward to a quiet evening alone. Now it looks like I'll be babysitting for two weeks.

Ten hours, five cups of coffee, and one very uncomfortable plane ride later, I'm on my way to Marcus's house. I swallow down the rest of my shitty cup of coffee just as the cab pulls up to a fucking mansion. Marcus said his job paid the bills, not that it paid for a goddamn castle.

I look down at my worn-out jeans and black T-shirt, both wrinkled from folding my six-foot-five-inch frame into the middle seat of the plane for four hours. I know for a fact my breath smells like the stale coffee I just drank, and my beard could use a trim.

The cabbie looks at me in the rearview mirror as if he's thinking the same thing I am. *Are you sure you belong here?*

I nod at him and hand the man my fare plus a tip before climbing out of the car and grabbing my duffel bag. The cab drives away, leaving me standing in front of the imposing double doors of my old military buddy's house.

My training kicks in and before I knock on the door, I scan the surrounding area. I'm not just looking for threats, I'm assessing the security that's already in place. How easy would it be for someone to break in?

I study the fence surrounding the grand estate, then the cameras that are angled toward the driveway. I make a note to talk to everyone who has access to the footage before turning my attention to the windows to look for potential points of entry.

The house itself is immaculate, with washed brick, a wraparound porch complete with a swing, several bay windows on the second floor with balconies of their own, and of course, huge double doors meant to intimidate and impress. And then there's the rest of the estate. A perfectly manicured lawn with trimmed hedges and a fountain with a weird little cherub-looking thing on top. I'll never understand rich people.

"Mr. Bennett?"

My head snaps in the direction of the sweetest voice I've ever heard.

There, standing in the front doorway, is a goddamn angel.

She's all soft curves, porcelain skin, and auburn hair. The angel even has on a white dress that flutters ever so slightly in the breeze. Her big brown eyes catch mine, staring right down into the depths of me. Why do I feel intensely vulnerable and ridiculously turned on by that? Is that a daisy woven into the long braid resting over her right shoulder? Who the hell is this creature?

My mind is spinning out of control as my heart crashes against my ribcage. What is she doing to me? Is this some sort of biological warfare? My hands start shaking so badly I have to ball them up into fists. Maybe it's all the coffee I had. Yeah, that must be it.

She parts her pretty pink lips to speak, and I realize who she is.

I leap up the three porch steps and storm toward the door, needing her to get to safety. I gently but firmly grip her shoulder, ignoring the shockwave crawling up my arm, and push her back inside the house before kicking the door closed.

"What the hell were you thinking?" I bark out. When the angel flinches, an unfamiliar feeling washes over me. I don't know what it is, but I don't think I like yelling at her.

"Are you my bodyguard?" she asks, blinking those doe eyes up at me. I realize I'm still holding onto her shoulder, so I let my hand drop as I take a step back. I ignore the hollow feeling in my chest at the loss of contact.

"You opened the door for a monster like me and you don't even know who I am?"

"You're not a monster!" she insists.

Her response draws out a humorless laugh from deep in my gut. "You don't know what I am, little girl."

*Shit, why did I say that?*

"Well, that's what I'm trying to get to the bottom of," she says exasperatedly, throwing her hands out in frustration.

I didn't realize until just now how small she is. And although she has generous curves I'm not letting myself look at, she's a tiny thing compared to me.

I take another step back when I get a whiff of her sweet scent. Crisp apples and honey. Is everything about this woman mouthwatering?

"Spencer." I grit her name out more harshly than I meant, but I need to get my head in the game. Getting lost in those chocolate brown eyes isn't doing anybody any favors. Wait, are those freckles? How many does she have? I want to count every single one of them and...

"No..." she draws out. "*I'm* Spencer. Who are you?"

The innocent, feisty little angel looks at me like I'm an idiot. I want to roll my eyes and also kiss that look off her face. Dammit.

"Logan Bennett," I finally answer.

"Ah-ha! I was right! You *are* my bodyguard!" Her satisfied little grin is almost worth the headache of our introduction, but I try not to dwell on that fact.

"You still shouldn't be opening the door for strangers." I fix her with a hard stare, but I hate every second of it. I don't like putting her in her place. I don't like glaring at her or scowling at her or any of the other ways I normally interact with people.

"But you just said—"

"In fact, you shouldn't be by the door at all," I continue. "What if I was your stalker?"

As soon as the words fall from my mouth I regret them.

Spencer's face pales and her bottom lip trembles. She dips her head down, looking at her feet as her shoulders slump.

Fuck, why does it physically pain me to see her like this?

"Spencer, I—"

I'm cut off by my cell phone ringing. Thank God. I don't know what I was about to say. I'm sorry? I don't think I've apologized since...well, I can't remember.

"Bennett," I answer the phone, though I never take my eyes off Spencer. Because of my job, not because I suddenly need to be in her presence at all times.

"Did you find the place alright? Is Spencer showing you around? I told her you were coming and to be on the lookout for a mean looking, tatted-up motherfucker with a heart of gold."

I grunt at Marcus, feeling the tiniest bit guilty for jumping down her throat when her own father told her to sit by the window and watch for me. I'll talk to him about that later when Spencer isn't right here.

"Just got here," I confirm. "Spencer is..." How do I even finish that sentence? She lifts her gaze, those deep brown eyes meeting mine. She chews on her bottom lip nervously as if hanging on my every word. "Good," I finally answer. "We're just getting to know each other."

The little angel gives me the briefest smile, her cheeks turning rosy before she averts her gaze. Christ, this is going to be a long two weeks.

# Chapter 2

*Spencer*

I'm already making a fool of myself in front of my new bodyguard, but I can't help it. I'm awkward on my best day, but when the sexiest man I've ever seen came bursting in the front door, my mind went to complete mush.

My dad said Logan Bennett was a big guy and had lots of tattoos, but that he served with Logan and knows he's a good guy. I trust my dad will protect me, and if he thinks Logan is the man for the job, then that's all I need to know.

I dart my eyes up to meet his briefly while he talks to my dad on the phone. I have to look away just as quickly because *good lord*, those eyes.

Ice blue and just as cold, but there's something more. Something deeper. Something I don't think even he understands about himself.

Or maybe I've just been cooped up in this house for too long.

My father has always been overprotective and I can't blame him. After the horrible car accident that took my mom's life and left me fighting for mine, it's understandable that he would want to keep an eye on me.

I had hoped he'd give me a little more freedom when I turned eighteen, but that only seemed to trigger more paranoia. He worried about me going off to college, so he convinced me to stay at home and take online courses.

It was a crushing blow, but I agreed like I always do. I so desperately wanted to move into the dorms and have friends and girls' nights and gossip until the early hours of the morning. I wanted to stay out late, eat too many carbs, and make rash decisions. I wanted to have an intelligent debate with my fellow classmates and be challenged by my teachers. All milestones I missed out on growing up.

It took several years of surgeries and recovery to fix my back and right leg, which delayed my schooling for a long time. Even after I was completely healed with only the scars to show, I never went to school or was allowed to hang out with kids my own age.

College was going to change all of that for me. Without my dad's financial backing, however, it wasn't going to happen. Plus, my dad was probably right when he told me it would be too much. I've been homeschooled my whole life and usually only leave home a few times a month to get art supplies and stop by my favorite coffee shop.

I get anxious—sometimes to the point of panic attacks—in crowds, small spaces, open spaces, and, well, pretty much all the time. Diving into the deep end with college would have been overwhelming.

Still, sometimes I wonder if he'll ever let me go. How will I know if I can fly on my own if my father never lets me spread my wings?

"I'll call with an update tonight," Logan grunts out, his eyes finding mine once more. It's like he can't help but look at me. I'm not much better; my eyes are drawn to him, too.

He hangs up and slips his phone into his back pocket, then stares at me expectantly.

"A tour!" I blurt out, spinning on my heel and walking through the foyer to the living room. I hear him grunt again as he follows closely behind.

For a big, muscled wall of a man, Logan is surprisingly light on his feet. I suppose being in the Marines and then running a security company taught him how to be stealthy.

I peer over my shoulder because apparently, I can't help myself. That beard. I don't know how I didn't notice it before. Well, okay, yes I do. It's because I was so distracted by the black ink swirling up his arms and his intense blue eyes.

But now that I'm looking...wow. I don't know why I love the scruffy beard, but I do. An image of his soft lips and scratchy beard trailing down my inner thigh pops into my head and I have to turn away from him.

*What is wrong with me?*

I've never entertained such thoughts. Being stuck at home for the last decade and a half didn't do me any favors in the relationship department, and I don't just mean having friends. The only guy I've talked to in the last few years, aside from my dad, is Mike from Freshly Brewed. He's at least a decade older than me and has been nothing but polite, if not a little aloof.

Logan has to be even older than Mike if he served with my dad in the military. That should probably stop my surprisingly dirty thoughts in their tracks, but it only seems to fuel the fire. I like that he's older. Experienced. Worldly. Maybe life wouldn't be so scary and overwhelming with someone like Logan by my side.

"Here's the couch," I say stupidly, just remembering I'm supposed to be giving him a tour. I look down at the blue velvet upholstery and wonder if I can sink into the cushions and hide until my embarrassment is over. "Uh, well one of the couches. It's my favorite because it has a great view of the hummingbird feeder. Did you know hummingbirds are the only birds that can fly backward? How cool is that? The average weight of a hummingbird is less than a nickel and they drink sugar water. That's probably why they can move so fast."

I have to bite the inside of my cheek to keep from rambling on and on about nothing. No, not nothing; I'm rambling about birds. Logan already thinks I'm an idiot for opening the front door, now he's going to know I'm a weirdo as well.

It feels good to have someone else to talk to, though, so I push through my anxiety and fight to stay in the moment. I'm mostly here at the house by myself since Dad has crazy hours at the office and travels a lot for work. I'm hard up for company these days, and my poor bodyguard now has to deal with my over-excitement and rambling stories.

Logan surprises me by stepping closer to the window and looking outside. I wonder if he finds the view as mesmerizing as I do. Even though I'm locked away here at home, at least the yard is gorgeous and attracts all kinds of beautiful birds and butterflies.

For a second, I think my bodyguard is looking intently at the cute pink hummingbird feeder with rhinestones and ribbons on it. I made it myself and the birds seem to like it. My dad shook his head when I hung it up, but I was so pleased with my project he didn't say anything.

Logan startles me by yanking the large curtains closed, turning back to me with a serious look in his eyes.

"No more standing by open windows," he declares as if his word is law.

"Excuse me?" I say, crossing my arms over my chest. Logan's eyes dip down, watching the motion for half a second before meeting my gaze again.

"For your safety. We still don't know much about this guy stalking you and I don't want to take any chances."

"Oh." When he puts it that way, it makes sense. But I still don't have to like it. I wrap my arms around myself now, no longer defensive. I just want a hug, but I don't have anyone to give one to me. As lame as it sounds, the birds are my only friends. If I can't see them, I'll be all alone.

"Maybe..." Logan's rough voice trails off and I look up, watching him rub the back of his neck. It seems like a nervous gesture, but I have no idea what someone like Logan would have to be nervous about. "Maybe there's a window facing the back of the property that would be safer," he offers.

"Yeah?" I say excitedly, hope blooming in my chest. "The one in my craft room faces the backyard and there's a high wall and thick forest, so no one can see in."

Logan's blue eyes never leave mine. I swear I see them soften ever so much, but maybe I'm just reading into it what I want.

"Show me." His voice is deep and gravelly, and I feel it travel through my body, sparking my nerve endings.

I nod and spin around again, unsure what to do with these strange feelings he's bringing out in me. I continue through the living room and down the hallway toward the right wing of our enormous house.

"Um, so this is the right wing of the house," I say with an unsteady voice, remembering once again I'm supposed to be showing him around. My hand swirls around in the air, pointing to everything and nothing. I'm a great tour guide. "My rooms are on this side."

"Rooms?"

"Bedroom, craft room, my office where I do schoolwork, bathroom, and a spare room in case I have a guest." I snort at the idea of me having a friend who would want to spend the night. Although now I'm glad there's an extra bedroom for Logan to sleep in. I don't think I want him very far away from me, especially with all the weird stuff happening lately.

I realize Logan has stopped walking, so I stop and turn as well. He's looking at one of my paintings I hung in the hallway. I debated whether I wanted to display something so personal, but in the end, it's not like anyone is going to see it anyway.

My dad doesn't come over to my side of the house often since he's rarely ever home anyway. And when he does, he never comments about my art projects. I think I remind him too much of my mom with my auburn hair and love of painting and crafts of all kinds. I remember helping her with her scrapbooking as a young girl. I'm pretty sure I just made more of a mess for her to clean up later, but I loved every second.

"I like it," Logan says. He sounds surprised at his admission, which makes it all the more genuine.

"Thanks," I say quietly, tucking some of my hair behind my ear.

Logan turns slowly, those otherworldly eyes of his resting on me once more. "You did this?" he asks, almost in awe. I nod my head.

He studies me intently, like he's trying to pick me apart and find out where I hid all the darkness to create something like that.

Admittedly, most of my artwork has bright colors and a healthy amount of glitter, but this one...well, it needed to be painted.

I look over his shoulder at the canvas with broad, abstract strokes of black paint that twist up into a million tree limbs. Two bright lights shine through the branches like headlights and deep red paint streaks across the lower left corner of the canvas.

Dark purple, black, deep brown, and forest green splash across half of the canvas and drip down. The colors mingle into an ugly mess before dripping right off the edge. It's a bit surrealist, which isn't my style at all, but everything that painting represents is surreal to me.

I know what this artwork means to me, but I wonder what he sees. I wonder what it makes him feel and which part made him react so strongly. Logan doesn't seem like the type of guy to comment on art, so this had to have meant something to him, right?

He clears his throat and looks away from me, letting me know we should keep going with the tour. Probably a good idea. If we stayed here any longer I'd end up rapid-firing my questions at him. After the hummingbird soliloquy, I figure it's best to give him a few hours to recuperate. I get the feeling Logan is the stoic, broody type.

We make it a few more steps down the hall before Logan stops again to look at another of my paintings. This one is pretty much the complete opposite. A little chickadee is happily chirping from a tree branch with a meadow of wildflowers in the background. The painting is done mostly in pastels, and not at all something a giant, tattooed, ex-military man would be interested in.

Logan looks at me, quirking up an eyebrow, silently asking if I did this one, too.

I nod and can't help the blush creeping into my cheeks. No one has ever seen my paintings, let alone complimented them.

Once again, we share a moment. Our eyes lock and all the differences between us fade away. Logan furrows his brow in concentration, then lets his gaze wander all around my face like he's trying to memorize me.

I take the opportunity to do the same.

Logan has sharp, angular features, although his nose looks like it's been broken a time or two. It somehow fits him perfectly, though. His midnight black hair is shorter on the sides and longer on top, perfectly blending into that beard of his I love so much.

He's got muscles on muscles, though not the bulky kind that come from the gym. No, this man is one hundred percent authentic. Those toned muscles were perfected from years of hard, manual labor. I watch his biceps and forearms flex, then look away, not sure what to do with the feelings rushing through my body.

My gaze travels up his body until I'm staring at his mouth. I don't know for sure, but his lips look soft. I can't stop thinking about kissing him and finally feeling what it's like to be wanted and desired that way.

When I meet his eyes again, it all becomes too much.

My heart thuds painfully in my chest and I feel my brow and upper lip break out into a cold sweat. Anxiety is a bitch.

"I have to pee!" I exclaim like a toddler. I cringe at my awkwardness, then turn on my heel and run down the hallway.

"Wait!" Logan calls out. "What about the window?"

"It's in there," I say, pointing to my craft room as I fly on by. "Sorry, can't hold it," I blurt out for some reason.

*Ohmygod, stop talking about going to the bathroom!* I don't even have to go; I just need to get away.

As I open the door to the bathroom, I give Logan one last look. He's still standing in front of my chickadee painting, gaping at me. I don't blame him. That was one hell of an introduction.

# Chapter 3

*Logan*

Ten minutes. That's all it took for me to become obsessed with the brown-eyed angel.

It's the way she nervously tucked her hair behind her ear, her sweet little blush, those damn curves I'd love to get my hands on. But there's more.

Spencer appears shy and innocent, and I have no doubt she is in every way, but there's a depth to her endless brown eyes beyond her twenty years. A sadness so great she had to put it on canvas.

Everything about this house is elegant and extravagant in ways I've never experienced. Marbled floors, extravagant vases, rugs that look too fancy to walk on, and even a statue of a medieval soldier in full armor. I mean, why the hell would anyone need that?

The decor made Spencer's dark painting stand out all the more. Angry black strokes littered the canvas and curled up into menacing trees. I have no idea how she managed to paint menacing trees, but that's exactly what they were.

The colors she used didn't exactly match, yet somehow that added to the chaos and devastation represented on the canvas. Coupled with the blood red drops and twisted trees, the painting felt like tearing open an old wound that never healed quite right.

Something about it hit me square in the chest. I somehow felt seen and understood in a way I didn't know I needed. The pain she spilled all over the canvas echoed my own in more ways than one. Turmoil, madness, and resignation bled from her art, as well as a quite kind of acceptance.

There was such raw fear, suffering, and overwhelming grief in that painting. A contrast to the bright, if not a bit skittish woman who painted it was jarring.

What happened to her? Spencer's father told me her mother died in a car accident, and I could see some of that represented in her painting. There was so much more to it, though.

I don't know shit about art, but I felt that painting deep in my soul. I didn't think I had one of those, but Spencer is proving me wrong every step of the way. The curvy angel has sparked something inside me, opening up a space I know only she can fill. I ache for this woman I barely know.

The other painting, the one with the bird and happy colors, seems more her style. Yet one look in those deep brown eyes said it all. She's both light and dark. Sweetness and sadness. Beauty and pain.

"Stop this shit," I grumble to myself as I lay here in bed. But I know it's no use. I haven't been able to stop thinking about her since she sprinted away from me hours ago.

I rub my eyes and take a deep breath, rolling onto my back. I can't help but picture her white dress as it kicked up behind her, showing me those creamy thighs. Christ, my dick is rock solid just thinking about what they would look like wrapped around my head.

My hand trails down my stomach and rubs the bulge in my boxers. I tip my head back and hiss at the contact. I've never had this instant, insatiable reaction to someone before, let alone a woman eighteen years my junior.

And let's not forget the fact that her dad is my old military buddy. What kind of asshole does that make me? I should be ashamed of myself.

My body doesn't seem to give a fuck, however.

When she looked at me over her shoulder, I swear I saw a longing in her eyes that matched my own.

I waited around in the hallway for a few minutes, noting that she didn't use the restroom or even pretend to flush the toilet or wash her hands. Creepy? Probably, but I take my duties as a bodyguard seriously. Especially when it comes to Spencer.

When she opened the bathroom door, I ducked into her craft room, which gave me the perfect angle to watch her without being seen. Spencer poked her head out and looked around, presumably for me. She blew out a huge breath and then muttered to herself, shaking her head before slipping into what I assume was her room.

She's complicated, that's for sure. I don't know why she felt the need to hide, but I gave her space for the rest of the day. God knows I can relate to wanting some alone time.

I spent the afternoon and evening getting my bearings around the huge estate, including a walk around the perimeter. I checked out the window in her craft room from the inside as well as the outside.

When I told her she can't stand in front of the windows anymore, her defiant edge surfaced, making my dick twitch for the first time in years. But then her shoulders slumped and she folded in on herself.

For the first time in my life, I caved. Windows make her happy and for some reason, her happiness has become my new priority. Second only to her safety.

Dammit.

I groan and throw the covers off, sitting up in bed and running my hands through my hair. My cock is throbbing and my thoughts are racing. This girl is messing with my head and making me want things I don't deserve.

She's also making me feel things I haven't felt in so goddamn long. I can't remember the last time I slept with someone. Ten years? Twelve? Even then, I'm sure it was nothing of note. I'm not the relationship kind of guy, but something about Spencer makes me want to try.

"Fuck," I grunt, tugging roughly at my hair as if I could somehow pull the thoughts of her from my mind.

I stand up and grab some clean clothes and a towel. A cold shower might help clear my head. I hope. I don't know how I'm going to stay under the same roof as the goddess with auburn hair, sad brown eyes, and a smile that lights up the room.

It's nearly midnight and I hope I'm not waking Spencer up, but I need to get this infatuation, or whatever it is, under control.

Cold water beats down on my back and I try to concentrate on all the things I need to do tomorrow. Starting with finding out more about Spencer's stalker and what exactly has been happening.

The thought of anyone harming her, scaring her, or hell, even looking at the precious angel the wrong way has anger burning a hole through my chest. I haven't killed anyone since my last tour ended years ago, but if some fucker came after Spencer on my watch, I might make an exception.

There's no doubt about it, this case is becoming far too personal, but I'm in too deep now. There's no going back.

Images of Spencer's delicate features sprinkled with freckles float into my mind, despite my best efforts. My thoughts wander to when she crossed her arms, pushing up her full, round tits. She wasn't even aware she was doing it, but my unruly cock sure did.

I bite back a groan, then look down at my solid erection. It hasn't gone down at all, and now it's angry. I shouldn't be indulging in the fantasy, but if I'm going to spend two weeks around her, I have to relieve this tension somehow.

I grab my thick shaft, gripping the base and stroking up and down, picturing Spencer on her knees in front of me. She looks up at me with those stunning brown eyes of hers and wraps her mouth around the monster between my legs.

I imagine her eyes fluttering closed, those long lashes fanning out over her delicate cheeks as she chokes around my girth. I grunt, possibly a little too loudly.

I continue to stroke faster, working myself up right to the edge just imagining her soft curves and pouty lips. In my fantasy, Spencer pinches her nipple and then slides her hand down her body, dipping her fingers into her soaking wet cunt.

She rubs her little clit, moaning as she gets herself off while sucking on my dick. Christ, what that does to me. I start trembling at the vivid picture in my mind.

Squeezing my dick, I pump my fist up and down in rough strokes, the intensity of my orgasm clawing down my spine. I picture pinning Spencer against the wall of the shower, her legs gripping my hips as I slam into her again and again.

I imagine her throwing her head back and crying out as I rut into her and then lean down and suck her hard nipple. I swear I can almost feel her walls starting to pulse around me as I draw out our pleasure. She shakes in my arms and I grip her ass tighter, pumping her body up and down my cock.

A glimpse of her pure, ethereal face twisted up in pleasure as she screams my name flashes through my mind and I lose it.

I shoot my cum all over the shower wall, rope after rope. Still trembling, I reach out a hand on the wall to steady myself as my cum keeps shooting out of me.

There's a soft gasp and I manage to turn my head in the direction of the sound, though I don't stop stroking myself.

My eyes lock onto a stunned Spencer, staring at me through the glass shower door. I'm a sick fuck, but I rub my dick raw and come again. Her eyes drop to my hand as it pumps up and down.

The siren licks her lips, making me growl.

Spencer gasps again, her cheeks turning bright red now. "I-I'm...sorry, I just needed to use the...never mind. I don't know why I keep talking about bathroom stuff," she sputters, her eyes never leaving my sore fucking cock. "Um, so...that's your, uh...wow, you're so big." Spencer covers her face with her hands and turns away from me, giving me her back. "Anyway, so, right. I'll use one of the other dozen bathrooms. Okay. Yup. See you tomorrow."

With that, she runs away from me for the second time today. We'll have to work on that in the future. Not that we have a future together, I just mean for these next two weeks.

*Yeah, keep telling yourself that.*

# Chapter 4

*Spencer*

I wake up in a sweat, my body tingling and shaking slightly from the vivid dream I just had starring none other than my sexy bodyguard. I have to rub my thighs together to try and ease the throbbing ache between them, but just like every other morning these last five days, nothing helps.

I shouldn't have walked in on him in the bathroom. I shouldn't have stared at him. I certainly shouldn't have drooled over his huge dick, but come on. I mean, I don't have any experience with guys, and I've never seen that particular part of their anatomy before, but God, there's no way that's average.

His ice-blue eyes locked on mine as he made himself come, and damn if that wasn't the hottest thing I've ever seen, let alone experienced.

Was he thinking of me? Part of me knows I should be scandalized, but I secretly love the thought of him being as attracted to me as I am to him. And lordy, I'm certainly attracted. More than attracted, I'm nearly obsessed with the man.

He's been professional since that night. Neither one of us has mentioned it, though I still blush pretty much any time Logan walks into the room. Sometimes I swear he smirks back at me, but it's always gone before I can be sure.

I'm sure he's bored out of his mind. So far he's watched me take my online classes, read, draw, and bake. Every few hours Logan does a perimeter check around the property, which I'm thankful for. It gives me a chance to breathe and fan myself.

My stoic bodyguard has barely spoken ten words to me since the shower incident, but I've learned an incredible amount about him just by being in his presence.

Logan never lets his guard down. He's always on the lookout for danger, always ready to strike. Sure, he was hired to protect me, so that makes sense. But I get the feeling he's like this even off duty. It makes me wonder the last time he relaxed, if ever.

He's also surprisingly orderly. I didn't expect that of a bearded man with tattoos crawling up his arms. I happen to know his chest and back are littered with ink as well, but I'm trying really, *really* hard not to think about that.

Maybe it's from his time in the military, but Logan likes to keep things neat and tidy. I went into his room one day to grab my crochet supplies that I keep in the closet and couldn't help but notice his bed was made to perfection. His clothes were hung up in the closet as well, even though they were mostly jeans and T-shirts. All of his personal possessions, which weren't much, were lined up in a straight line on the dresser.

I don't think I've ever been in a cleaner, more orderly room in my life. My craft room must give the man a headache. I can't remember the last time I organized my drawers and bins of supplies.

Aside from tense and orderly, I can sense that Logan is lonely. He'd never admit that, of course, but I recognize it all the same. I've been lonely for most of my life, but being with Logan makes me feel...seen. I hope I make him feel the same way, but Logan only has two facial expressions, stern and neutral, so it's hard to tell.

Sunlight peeks through the yellow curtains in my room, though it's still faint. I roll over and look at my phone. Six thirty in the morning. Not too bad, considering the first night Logan was here I didn't sleep at all.

I flop over onto my back and pull the covers over my head, but it's no use. The longer I stay in bed, the more I'm going to think about how much I wish Logan were here with me. And that's not going to help my situation whatsoever.

Sighing, I throw the covers off and sit on the edge of my bed, rubbing the sleep away from my eyes. I might as well make the most of my new early morning schedule if this is going to be a regular thing.

After throwing on a pair of leggings and a baggy sweatshirt, I decide to head to my craft room and work on a collage. I dig through a drawer filled with old magazines and pick out a few winners, then gather the rest of my supplies.

Ten minutes later, I have a poster board, Sharpies, glitter, glue, and a myriad of other embellishments. Whenever I'm feeling uninspired or stuck creatively, making a collage always seems to help. I'm hoping it will distract me from my decidedly dirty thoughts about the totally off-limits man sleeping two doors down.

I look up, noticing two cute little chickadees eating breakfast from my bird feeder right outside the window. Logan approved the blinds to be open in this room. He even surprised me by collecting my ten bird feeders around the property and placing them out back where I could still see them.

I'm not sure how he knew I loved my birds so much and would miss them if I couldn't see them every day. Maybe I'm not the only one who has been paying attention these last few days.

Getting up from my chair, I wipe my glitter-covered hands on my ratty old sweatshirt and head to the window to greet my guests.

"Hello, friends," I say softly, even though I know they can't hear me through the window. I realize I sound like a crazy person, or perhaps a pathetic person, but I owe a lot to my feathered friends. They've been here for me on some pretty dark days.

The cute little birds look up from the feeder. The female tilts her head to the side and looks at me before going back to her breakfast. The male chirps happily a few times, making me smile.

"Good morning to you, too, mister. Aren't you handsome?"

Just then, the door to my craft room swings open and bangs against the wall.

"Who the hell are you talking to?" Logan bellows.

I gasp and spin around, but my foot gets caught in one of the skeins of yarn I left out yesterday. I flail my arms out as I start to go down. Logan somehow appears right next to me, his strong arms gripping my shoulders as he hauls me up and steadies me.

I crane my head way back and look up into those piercing blue eyes. It's the first time we've looked at each other directly since his first night here and God...how is he more attractive now than he was then? I'm definitely going to be having naughty dreams about him tonight.

Just like that first day when he asked about my paintings, Logan studies every single thing about me, though his eyes never leave mine. I'm all too aware of the fact that his hands are still on my shoulders. They slowly slide down my arms, tickling my skin along the way, even through the sweatshirt I'm wearing.

My lips part on their own, and I find myself leaning into him. Logan dips his head, his hands still making their way down my arms until I feel his fingers wrap around my wrists. They stop just short of touching my skin, almost like he doesn't trust himself to take things any further.

Crazy, I know. There's no way this sexy beast is into someone like me. He's older, experienced, rough around the edges, and exudes control and authority. Not to mention I'm sure he breaks hearts and melts panties wherever he goes.

But the way he's looking at me right now, I'd almost think...

Logan clears his throat and drops his hands from my arms, taking a step back. He lifts one hand to rub the back of his neck—a nervous gesture I've seen him do a few times over the last few days—but then stops.

"What the..." He holds one hand out and then the other, palms up. "What is this?"

Logan stares at his hands, which are covered in the glitter I wiped off my own hands a few moments ago.

"Glitter," I say as if it's obvious.

He looks up at me, then back down at his hands. "Where did you get it?"

I try to hold back my grin, but it's too big. "From right here," I reply, pointing to the five containers of glitter on my table.

He grunts, studying the different colors. "I didn't know you could buy it like that."

My grin turns into a full-on cheesy smile. My big, bearded bodyguard has sparkly hands and looks bewildered by the loose glitter I purchased for three bucks at the local craft store.

"How do you normally buy your glitter?" I ask, feeling sassy. I don't know where it comes from, but I like teasing him.

Logan turns his head so he's looking right at me. And then his lips spread into the most beautiful, playful smile in the world. The intense features of his face soften. Even his eyes seem to change from cold to warm, like the ice is starting to melt.

"Can't say I've ever purchased glitter in any form, but when I do, I'll make sure to call and get your opinion."

I can't help but giggle. The thought of Logan in a craft store, talking to me on the phone while poring over the glitter options is both silly and sweet.

He gets another new, strange look on his face, though this one is harder to place. "What?" I ask self-consciously.

"I like your laugh." His eyes go wide, and I think he's about as shocked at his admission as I am.

"Thanks," I whisper. "I think I'd like yours, too."

Logan stares at me for a second, then opens his mouth. He closes it again, then furrows his brow and shakes his head. He takes another step back from me, and my heart sinks. Did I do something wrong?

He mumbles something about washing his hands, then hightails it out of the room.

Well, crap. I've run away from him twice, and now that he's done the same, I must say I don't like it. Not one bit.

# Chapter 5

*Logan*

"Fuck," I mutter to myself as I scrub pink and purple glitter off my hands.

I shouldn't have scared her. I shouldn't have held her. I shouldn't have stared into those deep brown eyes. I definitely shouldn't have let her know how intoxicating she is by just breathing the same air as me, let alone blessing me with her laughter.

But I can't help it.

I was getting dressed when I heard Spencer tell someone good morning and call them handsome. Anger and jealousy choked me up and dragged me out of the room, down the hall, until I burst into her craft room and scared the shit out of her.

She was talking to the birds. Of course she was. Spencer is as pure and sweet as the chickadees she loves so much. I'm a dirty old man for wanting to corrupt her.

The last of the sparkly shit finally washes down the drain, though I have a feeling I'll be finding more of it on my clothes for the rest of the day.

I splash some cold water on my face then blow out a breath. "She's off-limits," I remind myself. I go through the list of reasons why Spencer can't be mine. She's too damn young, for starters. I'm friends with her dad for fuck's sake. She's an innocent little lamb and I'm the big bad wolf who can't wait to sink my teeth into her soft, creamy skin.

Jesus, even as I'm trying to convince myself I'm no good for her, my dick is hard just thinking about biting and licking every inch of her curvy little body. I squeeze the fucker through my jeans, nearly coming with the vision of burying my face between her thighs.

"Goddamnit," I grunt, gripping the side of the sink with both hands so hard I'm afraid I might break the damn thing.

I take a deep breath and scrub a hand down my face. Today is day five of being Spencer's bodyguard. Five days of pure torture following the little angel around but not touching her. Not kissing those pouty pink lips. Not wrapping her up in a blanket and holding her until all the sadness is gone from wherever she keeps it locked up deep inside.

None of that is like me. I don't chase women. I don't obsess over them. I certainly don't cuddle them. But with Spencer...

I shake my head, clearing thoughts of a future with Spencer. I'm not the man for her. I'll be out of her life in a little over a week when her dad gets back from his business trip.

Ignoring the searing pain ripping through my heart at the thought of leaving her, I open the door and step outside into the hallway.

I've mostly gotten myself under control by the time I reach her craft room.

Peeking my head inside, I stop short, my breath catching in my throat.

Spencer is sitting at her desk, colorful art supplies strewn about her haphazardly, looking out the window with the softest smile on her face. The early morning sunlight shines on her face, lighting up little dust particles in the air and making her sparkle brighter than the glitter I just washed off my hands.

Her auburn hair looks almost fiery red in the orange glow of the sunrise. I want to run my fingers through those silky locks and see if she smells as sweet as she looks.

When Spencer turns to look at me, I swear to fucking Christ my heart stops and my chest caves in.

And then she smiles at me.

Fucking game over.

How can I resist her when she smiles at me and blushes?

My feet start moving before my brain can catch up. Her eyes follow me as I walk closer to her and lean against the wall next to the window.

It gives me the perfect view of her delicate features lit up by the first few rays of sunshine.

She's beautiful in a way I don't understand. My chest grows tight the longer she looks at me. She's studying me the same way I've been studying her these last few days. I wonder what she sees. A gruff, washed-up, bitter man? A lethal motherfucker with the scars to prove it? A desperate man in need of her touch, her smile, her light?

She'd be right on all accounts.

"You can sit down, you know," the little angel teases. "I won't bite."

Jesus, it takes everything in me not to groan at her words. She has no idea how much I want her to bite me. I want her mark on every part of me.

Spencer taps the leg of the chair next to me, scooting it a few inches closer to me. How can I deny her anything when she grins at me like that?

I sit down next to her, though I'm too tall to fit my legs under the table. Not that there's much room for me between the magazines, markers, ribbon, and of course, glitter. She's a beautiful mess and I want her as mine. Fuck that, I *need* her.

"What are you making?" I grunt out, wincing at my harsh tone.

Spencer just keeps right on smiling at me before looking around at the chaos surrounding her. Normally, a mess like this would frustrate me endlessly, but how can I be upset when Spencer looks so happy?

"A collage."

When I don't respond, she looks up at me again, then quickly drops her eyes to the table. She picks up one of the magazines and flips through it, landing on a page with a picture of a meadow on it. It's an ad for some allergy medicine, but Spencer cuts just the meadow part out, then arranges it on the poster board to her liking.

Watching her work is...soothing. I can't explain it and I don't want to. Spencer is pure light and magic. That's all there is to it.

"What is it for?" I find myself asking. I want to hear her voice again. Need it in a way that terrifies me and excites me at the same time.

Her hands stop moving and then she slowly lifts her head, tilting it to the side as she stares at me.

"You want to know about my art?" God, the doubt in her soft tone kills me.

How do I tell her I'd listen to her talk about paint drying or migration patterns of the birds she loves so much or any and every thought that pops into her head?

I don't want to open my mouth in case any of those words come out, so I nod.

Her eyes sparkle, the little golden flecks in her irises shining with delight. Am I the reason for her joy? I can't be, but part of me hopes so. I must have done something incredible in a former life to be here in this moment with Spencer.

"Well," she says, clasping her hands together as she launches into a graduate level course lecture on collages. "For me, collages are kind of like a mood board..."

I sink further into my seat, letting her voice seep into my skin. I feel it coursing through my veins and wrapping itself around my heart, branding me for all of time. This woman has a hold on me. I have a feeling she already owns me, body and soul.

The snapping of a branch jars me out of my relaxed state. I don't think I've ever felt that good and she was only talking to me.

But now I'm on high alert, every one of my protective instincts kicking in.

"What's wrong?" Spencer whispers, her eyes darting around the room.

I jump up from my chair, nearly knocking it over as I peer out the window. I see the bushes lining the far wall rustle ever so slightly, making my fists clench at my sides. Anger and adrenaline flood my system, snapping me back into bodyguard mode.

"Go into the bathroom and lock the door," I growl at her. When she flinches away from me I want to punch myself in the face. I don't know how to be gentle, but fuck, I want to try. "Everything will be okay," I tell her, trying to make my voice softer.

She nods once, swallowing back her fear. Spencer trembles slightly and she looks white as a fucking sheet, but she obeys.

I go into my room and grab the gun I keep in the bedside table drawer, tucking it into the waistband of my jeans and covering it with my shirt. I move quickly and quietly through the house, slipping out one of the doors that leads to the backyard.

Keeping close to the wall surrounding the property, I carefully do a perimeter sweep, starting with the bushes that were moving a few moments ago.

I get there just in time to hear a thud on the other side of the wall, then footsteps pounding the pavement. Without hesitating, I back up a few feet then run at the six-foot-tall wall, grabbing the top of it as my right foot kicks off the solid brick, giving me a boost. Pulling myself up, I leap over the top and hit the ground, rolling once before righting myself.

I see a tall man in all black sprinting down the private road on the backside of the property. I take off after him, adrenaline fueling every step. I must eliminate the threat.

The man cuts a sharp right onto the main road. I follow him, desperate to close the gap between us. He stops in front of a black car parked off to the side, partially hidden by a tree. I push myself to reach him before he opens the door, but it's too late.

He climbs into the car and takes off, tires squealing and leaving behind the smell of burning rubber. I chase it for a good fifty feet, but it's no use. At least I got the license plate number.

I wipe a hand down my face, catching my breath before scanning the area for any more clues. Spencer and I haven't talked much over the last few days, and her father is being dodgy every time I call him for a check-in.

I don't think Marcus is behind this. He's not capable of harming his daughter. However, I do think he knows more than he's telling me. I'll get to the bottom of it, but for now, I have to move Spencer to a safe house.

On my way back to the house, I call the Watchdog Protection office, getting Colton on the line. He may come off as someone who goofs around too much, but the man is serious about the important things. In fact, the fucker is downright lethal when pushed to the edge. He also knows everyone and has what feels like unlimited connections.

In under five minutes, Colton has located a safe house a few hours away, courtesy of one of his many contacts. If I didn't know he was such a solid guy, I'd think Colton was shady as fuck. As it is, I'm glad to have him part of my team.

After giving Marcus an update via text, I finally head back inside to check on Spencer. The poor girl looked absolutely terrified, but at least I know she's safe. The fucker didn't get near the house and I'm taking her away from here. I have to keep reminding myself of that as I walk down the hall and knock on the bathroom door.

"Spencer?" I ask, trying to be calm and soothing for her.

When all I hear is a shuddering breath, I snap, swinging the door open to make sure she's okay. What I see absolutely guts me.

Spencer is standing in the far corner, leaning back against the wall. Her eyes are rimmed in red, tears staining her pale cheeks. She's whimpering and shaking almost violently, her breath shallow and choppy. Spencer has her arms wrapped around her middle like she's trying to hold herself together.

"What's wrong?" I demand, taking a few steps closer to her.

"I-I-I..." she hiccups as more tears spill over onto her cheeks. "D-don't...like...s-small spaces," she manages to stutter out in-between her frantic gasps for air. "Panic attack," she adds, her voice barely above a whisper.

I close the distance between us, though I stop short of touching her. I don't want to crowd her, but I'm not sure what to do. Fuck, how do I make it better?

"What can I do? What helps?"

The terrified, trembling angel looks up at me, those brown eyes of hers pleading with me to make it better, to take her fear away.

"Compression," she whispers.

"Compression?" Spencer nods then squeezes her arms around her middle. Suddenly it clicks. "A hug?" She sniffs miserably and then nods her head again.

I've never hugged anyone before, but that doesn't seem to matter. She's wrapped up in my arms in the next second.

# Chapter 6

*Spencer*

Logan holds me close, his whiskey and pine scent filling my lungs and calming me down ever so much.

He's so freaking huge his body completely engulfs mine in the warmest, most comforting hug I've ever had. I bury my face into his chest, wanting to be closer somehow. Logan tightens his hold on me, surrounding me with his strength.

"Am I doing it right?" he asks softly.

Despite my pounding heart and racing thoughts, I find my lips pulling into a smile. The beastly bodyguard is surprisingly sweet.

I nod as I cling to him, letting his steady breath and the beat of his heart bring me back from the edge of fear. He strokes my back, his fingers gliding up and down my spine. I didn't think Logan was capable of being so gentle, but here he is, holding me like I'm the most precious thing in the world.

I take a moment to soak up everything he's giving me, then reluctantly pull back from him.

Logan drops his hands to my hips, still holding me close but letting me have some space. I look up at those severe blue eyes of his, surprised to see them full of worry. He stares at me for a long, heavy moment, then surprises me further by pressing his lips to my forehead.

Closing my eyes, I savor the feeling of his tender kiss. I have no idea what this means, only that I need it. I need *him*. Need him in a confusing, terrifying, all-consuming way that settles deep in my soul.

"I've got you," he murmurs onto my skin, pulling me into his arms once more.

I melt into his embrace as more tears pour down my cheeks. I don't even know why I'm crying, but it doesn't matter to Logan as he combs his fingers through my hair and gently rocks me back and forth. I've never felt so cherished.

*Can I stay here forever?*

Logan grunts and squeezes me tighter. "You can stay here as long as you want."

I should be embarrassed I said that out loud, but his response soothes my anxiety. Everything about this man soothes me. He'd protect me from anything and fight off my demons if I let him.

We stay like that for long moments until I stop shaking and can breathe normally again. This time when I step away, he lets me. Until my knees buckle, that is.

Logan scoops me up in his arms and I automatically curl up into his chest, burying my face into the side of his neck. He carries me into my room and gently sets me down on the comfy couch in the corner.

He stands back and runs his hands through his hair before looking around. "Stay," he grunts at me. I nod and watch him leave, tucking my legs under me as I curl up on the couch.

A few moments later, Logan has the big fleece blanket I keep in the living room for movie nights. I sit up slightly and reach out for it, touched that he remembered it's my favorite. Instead of handing the blanket to me, Logan drapes it over my shoulders and proceeds to wrap it tightly around me.

"Compression," he says, pulling it tighter and nodding with satisfaction. God, this man. He's ruining me. "What else? What can I do? Is there a list?" He looks at me expectantly, as if I have a checklist of things that make me feel better.

"No list," I whisper, not trusting my voice.

Logan's lips form a straight line and he grunts once more. "I'll work on one."

His response is so serious, so matter-of-fact, I have to smile. I like the idea of him having a list of things about me, no matter what it is.

"Maybe you could sit next to me?" I ask softly.

Logan immediately stops pacing and joins me on the couch. I lean against his arm, but Logan wants more than that. He pulls me into his lap, blanket and all as if I weigh nothing. My arms are trapped in the blanket cocoon, but I don't care. I don't feel suffocated, I feel safe and protected for the first time in so long.

After a few moments of silence, Logan clears his throat. "Why do small spaces give you panic attacks?" he murmurs.

"What happened outside?" I ask, avoiding his question.

"You answer me and I'll answer you," he says with the smallest little grin. I love it. I can't wait to see him smile for real and laugh.

Despite not wanting to think about that awful night, I find myself opening up to him and giving him this little piece of my heart.

"When I was five, my mom and I were in a car accident," I murmur, resting my head against his shoulder. Logan doesn't say anything, he just gives me space to tell my story. "It was late and rainy and she slipped off the road, hitting a tree head-on. She..." I choke on a sob, and Logan brushes away my tears before tucking my hair behind my ear.

"I've got you," he whispers for the second time today. I believe him.

We sit in silence for a few moments while I gather the strength to tell him more. I haven't talked about that night in years. My dad didn't know how to handle the grief of losing his wife while also taking care of a broken daughter.

At least he had the foresight to take me to a child psychologist so I could work through the emotional trauma and not just the physical trauma to my body. I've healed in a lot of ways in the last fifteen years, but those same fears and insecurities still follow me around.

I thought I'd always be damaged, but being right here in Logan's arms makes me feel complete. He's filling in the cracks of my heart and mending me in ways I didn't know I needed.

"She died on impact," I tell him, my voice growing stronger the more he holds me.

"I'm so sorry, sweetheart."

My chest grows tight and a blush creeps into my cheeks at his endearment. He keeps surprising me with his tender heart. I want to keep it as my own.

"I...I was trapped in the back seat." I shudder at the memory and slam my eyes shut against the onslaught of emotions clogging up my throat. I've come this far though, and I know I need to push through. "It was so dark and Mom was so silent," I whisper, remembering how completely alone I was.

The rain beating down on the car was the only sound I heard for what felt like an eternity. I went in and out of consciousness, each time startling awake, thinking it was a nightmare. The reality that greeted me when I opened my eyes only got worse and worse each time.

"I don't know how long we were out there before a car stopped and someone called the cops," I continue. "I overheard the police tell my dad it must have been hours, but I had no sense of time."

"Spencer," Logan murmurs, his voice carrying so much pain. He rubs my back in calming circles and kisses the top of my head.

"Firefighters had to cut me out of the car. I don't remember much after seeing a scary man in a suit and helmet wielding what looked like a giant pair of scissors. It was probably for the best. I woke up days later in the hospital after three surgeries. Once I recovered, I had two more surgeries on my back and one on my right leg before I was back to normal."

"How old were you after you healed from all the surgeries?"
"Eight."

Logan inhales sharply, his muscles tensing until he exhales. He tips my chin up, his blue eyes peering directly into mine. They take hold of me and I can't look away. He's studying me like he does every time we lock eyes, but this time he seems to find answers to the silent questions he's been asking himself.

"The painting," he whispers.

Tears burn my eyes as I nod once. I don't have to say anything more. He's seen the most painful parts of me, my darkest fears, my broken heart, and my loneliness. I put it all on that canvas, and it only drew Logan closer to me.

Slowly, so slowly, Logan dips his head down, rubbing his nose against mine. The simple gesture makes me feel so safe and treasured, while also making my skin tingle with awareness.

"You're so strong," he murmurs, his lips barely brushing mine. I can feel his warm breath tickle my lips, his blue eyes never leaving mine.

I shake my head no, rubbing my nose against his. Logan nods his head at the same time, making me smile.

Then he presses his lips to mine, applying the lightest pressure. My arms are still wrapped up in my blanket, but I tilt my head up, welcoming more of him.

Logan cups my face in one hand, angling me before parting my lips with his tongue. I gasp as he licks into my mouth, exploring me in long, languid strokes.

"Spencer," he says softly, almost in awe before claiming my lips once more.

His hand slides down to my neck, his thumb caressing my pulse point and making me whimper. Logan groans into the kiss, opening me up more, tangling his tongue with mine.

His fingers trail lower until they're tugging at the blanket. I help him, desperate to have my hands on more of this incredible man.

When I'm finally free, my hands go to his face, my fingers weaving in his scruffy beard and pulling him closer. God, how many times have I imagined this kiss? How many hours have I spent wondering what his beard would feel like on my skin while his soft lips trail over my body?

Logan groans, tearing his mouth from mine, only to litter kisses down my neck. I moan when I feel him nip at my sensitive skin and lick away the sting. He nuzzles into my shoulder, panting as heavily as I am.

I place a hand on the side of his cheek, my thumb stroking his skin in a featherlight touch. Logan lifts his head, his eyes roaming over my face before landing on mine.

"You taste so damn sweet," he murmurs before kissing my forehead.

"You're not so bad yourself," I tease, still catching my breath.

"I'm not sweet," comes his gruff reply.

"You are to me."

He stares at me for a long moment, his brows furrowed slightly. I can feel his vulnerability coursing through him. I want nothing more than to crawl inside his chest and pick up all the little pieces of his surprisingly fragile heart. I don't know what broke it, only that our jagged pieces will fit perfectly together.

# Chapter 7



*Logan*

I've never been called sweet, but when the word fell from Spencer's lips, I believed her. I'm a growly bastard to everyone else in my life, but this angel? She deserves all the sweetness and love I didn't know I was capable of.

Hold up.

*Love?*

"What's wrong?" Spencer asks, still caressing my cheek. How she can undo me with one touch I'll never know, but I'll gladly fall apart for her anytime.

"Nothing," I murmur, leaning in for another kiss. I don't have time to unpack my confusing feelings for this woman. Not when she's right here in my arms, begging me to kiss the breath right out of her lungs.

Spencer gasps softly before parting her lips and letting me have my fill. She surprises the hell out of me by sucking on my tongue and wrapping her arms around my neck like she can't get close enough.

I growl into her hot little mouth, unable to control my desperate need for this woman. Her breasts are crushed up against the hard planes of my chest, making my dick impossibly harder. I want to suck on her pebbled nipples, bite her supple flesh, and lick up her cleavage.

And then I want to slide my cock between her generous tits and fuck her there before tearing open her pussy.

Jesus, if she knew how depraved I am, she'd run in the opposite direction. Then again, the way my sweet little angel is rubbing up against me makes me think she'd be into it. I fucking hope so, because now that I've tasted her, felt her, swallowed down her wanton cries...I don't think I can let her go.

It takes every ounce of willpower to break our kiss and pull away from her, but I need to get her out of here. I won't compromise her safety just to get my dick wet. This girl deserves so much more than a quick fuck on the couch. She deserves everything. I just hope I'm lucky enough to be the man who gives it to her.

Spencer's chest is heaving as she catches her breath, her lips are swollen, and her face is flushed from the way we devoured each other. She's a vision. My wicked angel, equal parts innocence and pure sin. Temptation and salvation. A contradiction worthy of the woman herself, carrying around her light while harboring darkness deep in her soul.

She leans in for more, and God, do I want to give it to her. But not here. Not now.

"We have to stop, sweetheart," I tell her when she pouts at me. That's a dangerous look. It makes me want to put something between those swollen pink lips of hers.

"Why?" Her brown eyes are nearly black with lust, but I have to stay strong. "Oh. Outside..." She gasps softly, her muscles tensing up when she remembers why I wrapped her up in a blanket and held her in the first place.

"You're safe with me," I promise her, easing some of her fear. "Do you trust me? Trust that I'll protect you?"

"With all of me," Spencer answers immediately. Her words make me feel about ten feet tall, and I resist the urge to beat my chest like a victorious warrior. Damn if I don't feel like one, though.

"Then we need to pack you a bag and hit the road."

"What? Where? Why?"

I feel her start to panic, so I cup the back of her neck, massaging it lightly as I tip her head up. "Do you trust me?" I ask again, willing her to say yes. I don't think anyone is in the house, and I doubt the place is bugged, but I don't want to give any more information just in case. That's how stupid mistakes are made.

Spencer nods her head, leaning forward slightly to rub her nose against mine. Something about that feels so right, so comforting. Like home. Or like I imagine home would feel like. I've never experienced that before, but I feel it settle deep in my bones. Spencer is my home now.

I help her off my lap, groaning when she brushes against my throbbing erection. She looks at me over her shoulder and gives me the sexiest little grin. I swat her ass as she wiggles around on my lap, making her gasp and then laugh softly.

"Christ, woman, you're gonna be the death of me," I growl, leaning forward to suck on the sensitive spot beneath her ear.

Spencer hums in satisfaction, then hops off, leaving me wanting so much more. How can such a pure creature be so effortlessly seductive?

Twenty minutes later, we've finally loaded up the car and are on our way to a remote cabin near Sausalito, California.

I helped Spencer pack a small suitcase with clothes and toiletries, and then somehow found myself loading up two more suitcases with enough craft supplies to last a year. My resolve to only stick with the essentials crumbled when she turned those big brown eyes on me. There's nothing I would deny my angel. If she doesn't already know that, she will soon.

I merge onto the highway and set a steady speed toward the cabin in the woods. I'll take back roads once we get closer, but for now, we're hiding in plain sight, getting lost in traffic.

Spencer has been quiet this whole time. When I look over at her, she has her arms wrapped around herself again, looking out the window. Her silhouette glows in the morning light, drawing my attention to her button nose and full lips. I have to force my eyes back on the road, though it takes considerable effort.

I want to pull over, haul her curvy little body into my lap, and hug her. It seemed to help last time. I hate that she's been the only one to comfort herself these last few years. I get the sense her father hasn't been around that much. I'll have to talk to him about his absence. Marcus should have been there for his daughter. I suppose I can get it all out in the open when I tell him Spencer is mine now.

I reach out and gently stroke her left arm, coaxing her to unwrap it so I can lace our fingers together.

"It's going to be okay," I tell her softly. She nods but doesn't look at me.

I focus my attention on the road, trying to figure out a way to ease her anxiety. So far I know hugs, blankets, and possibly sitting on my lap helps, but I can't act on any of that right now.

"I don't know why this is happening," Spencer murmurs. "I don't know what I did or why I'm being targeted."

"You know none of this is your fault, right?"

"I'm not sure of anything anymore."

I can hear how tired she is, the defeat in her voice cracking my heart in two. I know today was a lot for her. First her panic attack, then telling me about her mom, followed by me practically mauling her...it's all catching up to her.

"This," I say, lifting our hands up and looking at her briefly. "You can be sure about this Us. We're solid, angel. I'm not going anywhere."

My eyes are back on the road, but I feel her little hand squeezing me right back. Spencer shuffles around in her seat, then scoots closer so her head is resting on my bicep. She melts against me and sighs so sweetly.

I must have said something right to get her to relax. I make a mental note to remind her regularly how much she means to me if it soothes her this much.

"I started getting letters about a month ago," she says softly.

I've wanted to ask her about her stalker since I first laid eyes on her, but between her running away from me and then us avoiding each other the last few days, I didn't get a chance. She's already spilled so much of her heart out today, and here she is, giving me more of her pain. I want it all. If I could carry her pain for her, I would. All I can do is share the weight of her burden and hopefully provide the strength she needs to heal once and for all.

"The first one was a poem. I found it on the front step when I went outside to fill up my bird feeders. The envelope just had my name on it, no address or stamp or anything."

So the fucker definitely knows where she lives. Why didn't Marcus tell me that? I would have insisted on taking her to a safe house from day one. I don't know what to do with this information, so I tuck it away for now.

"What did the poem say?"

"I had to look it up to be sure, but it's a line from a Pablo Neruda poem." She takes a breath before reciting the poem as if she's played it over and over in her head in the weeks since she received it. "You are here. Oh, you do not run away. You will answer me to the last cry. Curl round me as though you were frightened. Even so, a strange shadow once ran through your eyes."

Spencer shivers as the last word falls from her lips. I have no idea who this Pablo person is, but he must've been some sort of famous poet. Of course, Spencer would know something like that. A big brute like me? I can't say I've ever read a poem in my life.

"The poem is actually really romantic," she adds. "But not like this. I mean, who would send me something like that? I hardly talk to anyone except when I'm doing my online classes. Even then, I don't have my camera on or anything, so it's not like they can see me or any identifying things about my surroundings. It was one of the things my dad made me agree to in order to take classes in the first place."

I nod, taking in all of this information. So Marcus *is* protective of her, just not in the way she needs. Or maybe he's overprotective because he knows about some threat she doesn't.

"What else happened? Did you get any other notes?"

"Yeah, the next week there was a single rose tucked into the side of one of the bird feeders with a small note attached. It said..." She blows out a breath before continuing. "It said, 'You're like a flower. I can make you bloom for me or trample you underfoot. The choice is yours.'"

"Motherfucker," I growl, gripping the steering wheel with one hand while clutching Spencer with the other.

"So that's when I told my dad."

"What did he say?"

"He..." Spencer trails off, considering my question. "I guess I thought he would be more upset. He's so paranoid about everything where I'm concerned, but now that I think about it, he didn't look shocked. He looked...determined, I guess. I don't know. It's hard to read him sometimes."

I grunt in acknowledgment, gathering up more information to pick apart later.

After a few minutes of silence, I look over at Spencer, wanting her to continue. She yawns and snuggles deeper into my side, if that's possible. I want to hear more, but I can tell she's about to pass out from exhaustion.

"Close your eyes, sweetheart. Just a few more hours now." As if waiting for my permission, Spencer flutters her eyes closed. I smile to myself when I hear her soft snores.

Two hours later, I'm pulling into the safe house. It's a nice little cabin, plain and nondescript on the outside, which is perfect. If you didn't already know it was here, you'd probably miss it. The natural wood blends right into the thick forest surrounding us. I'll have to remember to thank Colton for finding this place, shady contacts or not.

Spencer woke up a few times during the road trip, but went back to sleep about thirty minutes ago, this time curling up on the other side of her seat. She's beautiful and precious and vulnerable, sleeping soundly right next to me. She's given me her trust and I'll never take that for granted.

I can't stop myself from reaching out and smoothing her hair behind her ear. My thumb trails over her cheek and jaw, and I marvel at how soft she is. This isn't the time nor the place, however. I need to get her inside to safety.

I shut off the car and quietly step out, shutting the door and locking the vehicle so Spencer is safe inside but can get out if she wakes up and panics.

After a quick sweep of the perimeter and the cabin, I come back out to the car and gently open Spencer's door, unbuckling her seatbelt and scooping her up into my arms. She automatically curls up against my chest, resting her head on my shoulder. Goddamn, it feels good to hold her again.

I carry her up the stairs, through the cabin, until I reach the bedroom. There's only one, which means I'll be folding my six and a half-foot frame onto the tiny couch in the living room, but that's alright. I've slept in worse places for far less worthy causes.

Pulling back the covers, I carefully set my sleeping angel down on the mattress before taking her shoes off and tucking her in. It's just past four in the afternoon, but Spencer needs her rest after the long day she had. Fuck, I need to sleep too, but I'm far too jacked up on adrenaline to sit still longer than I already did in the car, let alone close my eyes.

I stand beside the bed, watching over Spencer as she snuggles further into the blankets. So innocent, so fucking pure. And yet, there's an inner strength to this woman that rivals that of anyone I've ever met.

"Sweet dreams, angel," I whisper, leaning over to kiss her forehead. The softest little sigh leaves her lips, making my heart clench up tight. She likes forehead kisses and rubbing noses. I'll add that to the list of things that make her feel better.

Reluctantly, I make my way out of the bedroom, making sure to leave the door open a crack. I don't want her to feel trapped or wake up confused and thinking she's locked in the room.

While my girl sleeps soundly, I get to work researching Marcus and everyone he's done business with since he got out of the military. Something's not adding up and I intend to find out exactly what it is.

# Chapter 8

*Spencer*

I wake up in a pitch-black room with my heart hammering against my ribcage.

*Where am I? Did my stalker kidnap me? Oh God, what if I never see Logan again?*

Memories of yesterday come rushing back to me. Logan hugged me and calmed me down after my panic attack. He wrapped me up in a blanket and listened to me cry about my mom. And then he kissed me. Lord, did the man kiss me.

My cheeks heat up at the memory of his rough hands roaming over my body and tangling in my hair. The way his tongue slid against mine, his tortured groans as he took and took and took from me. I wanted him to have it all. Everything. I think I would have straddled the man and given him my virginity if he hadn't stopped us.

It finally hits me. I'm in the safe house.

I take a deep breath and release the tension in my muscles. Looking around the room, I try to locate an alarm clock or something to tell me what time it is.

I don't have my phone since Logan took out the SIM card and broke it into a million pieces before crushing the phone itself. I was shocked, to say the least, but then he explained he didn't want anyone to track me.

Sitting up in bed, I turn toward the lone window on the opposite wall. I can only see a hint of moonlight streaming through the thick forest outside. It must be late. I've probably slept for hours. The rumbling in my tummy confirms that I haven't eaten in a while.

I flop back down on the mattress and close my eyes, willing sleep to come. Every few seconds, however, I peek my eyes open and scan the room, looking for any monsters hiding in the shadows.

Ever since the car accident, I've been afraid of the dark. It's usually not crippling or anything like that, but I do sleep with a nightlight and sometimes leave a lamp on if I'm feeling particularly vulnerable. Add on to that a stalker I know next to nothing about, and yeah, I'm on edge and paranoid in this dark room.

I clench my fists and blow out another breath, then try counting down from one hundred, like my therapist taught me all those years ago. I'm at sixty eight when something scratches the window.

I pull the blankets over my head and cower under them, trying not to breathe. After a few seconds, the small space becomes suffocating. Slowly, so slowly, I pull the covers down, venturing a glance at the window.

Every muscle in my body relaxes when I see it's just a branch scratching the window as it's blown in the breeze.

"You're fine," I whisper to myself.

The branch scrapes against the window again and I jump, barely suppressing a whimper.

I throw the covers back and sit up. Maybe a glass of water would help. As much as I hate the idea of walking around the dark cabin, I'm going to drive myself crazy staying in here by myself with the scratchy window.

The door is slightly ajar, which I appreciate. Something tells me Logan did it on purpose. The man is nothing if not observant and detail oriented. Just one more reason to love him.

*Love?*

But it's true. I've always loved him. I don't know how or when it happened, exactly, but the thought of leaving this man is so painful I feel tears well up in my eyes. I'm crazy for having these thoughts, and certainly for having these intense feelings about Logan. I just hope I can convince him to love me as well.

Tiptoeing into the hallway, I'm relieved to see a faint light coming from what I assume is the living room. I walk in that direction, then stop when I see Logan's massive frame stretched out on the thick rug in front of the fireplace.

It looks like he tried sleeping on the couch, but of course he didn't fit. Guilt sits heavy in my stomach. I didn't know there was only one bed. Then again, I was passed out when Logan carried me inside, but still. He's worked so hard protecting me and chasing away the threat to my safety. He deserves to sleep in the bed.

Before I know what's happening, I'm shuffling toward him. I don't know what my plan is. Should I wake him up? Tell him to go sleep in the bed? It's not like he would agree to that anyway, I just know it.

I can't seem to walk away from him, though. It's like my body knows exactly where it belongs—beside this man forever.

Instead of intruding on his sleep to tell him my insane thoughts, I get down on the floor and carefully slip under the big blanket draped over his body. My fears instantly scatter in Logan's presence. Even in sleep, he's providing me comfort and safety.

I scoot a little closer to him, snuggling up against his side. Logan is lying on his back, one arm flung over his eyes, with the blanket halfway down his chest. His bare chest. His bare, sculpted, mouthwatering chest. I can't help but reach out and touch him.

My fingers trace over the swirls of black ink that crawl up his arms and over his pecs, trailing down one side of his ribcage. He's a work of art, inside and out.

I gently lay my cheek down on his chest, right over his heart. The steady rhythm echoes in my head, my heart, my entire being, lulling me to sleep.

Some low, gravelly sound reverberates deep inside Logan's chest, startling me awake.

"Spencer?" How is his scratchy, sleepy voice even sexier than his regular voice? "Are you okay?"

"I am now," I whisper, tilting my head up.

The dying embers from the fire cast an orange glow over Logan's severe features and light up his blue eyes. There's such concern there, as well as a hint of anger, but not at me. It's like he's already angry at whatever made me afraid, even though he has no idea why I came out here in the first place.

"Did something scare you?"

I look away from him, embarrassed to admit I freaked out over a tree branch. Logan cups the back of my neck, tilting my head up to meet his gaze once more.

"I'm not a fan of the dark," I whisper. His eyes go soft as he leans down to brush his nose against mine. Butterflies erupt in my tummy, flooding my body with an unexpected wave of lust. I'm all too aware of how close we are, how easy it would be to…

His lips are on mine in the next second like he could read my thoughts and my body better than I can.

I give myself over to him, letting him tease and taste and do whatever he wants to me. Each swipe of his tongue makes me shiver and clench my thighs together.

Logan groans and rolls me onto my back, leaning over me and kissing down my throat. I gasp and whimper when he tugs at the neckline of my shirt with his teeth.

"Logan," I breathe out, bowing my back and shoving my breasts closer to him. I can't explain it, but I need more. I don't even know what that means, but I want him to show me.

"What do you need, Spencer?" he murmurs into my skin.

"You," I moan as I wiggle my hips. It's like I can't stay still. There's too much lust, too much desire twisting me up inside. I need Logan to take care of me in the way only he can.

Without another word, Logan leans back and lifts my shirt over my head. He takes my wrists in one hand and guides them over my head again.

"Keep these here for me."

I give him a questioning look. He smiles and leans down, brushing the shell of my ear with his nose and lips. "Trust me, you'll like it." Logan nuzzles my neck and kisses a trail over my collarbone and between my breasts. "Goddamn, sweetheart. I could live right here, buried in your gorgeous tits."

He kisses one breast and licks my nipple before sucking it into his mouth. Logan groans, the sound equal parts torture and relief. He continues licking around my nipple and then bites the hard bud.

My back arches off the floor and I let out a sharp cry that turns into a moan.

He looks up and me from between my breasts. "Did you like that, baby?"

I nod, unable to form words.

My beastly bodyguard growls and holds my other breast in his palm, kneading and caressing my sensitive flesh. When he bites one nipple and pinches the other, I feel the jolt zip through my body all the way down to my clit. My hips jerk up, rubbing against his hard length.

Logan keeps his mouth on my skin, sucking, nipping, and kissing around my breasts while his right hand trails further down my body. He slips his fingers into my leggings, rubbing my aching pussy. My hips involuntarily thrust upward, trying to get some relief.

"Please," I whisper, my breath caught in my throat.

Logan chuckles darkly, then slowly slides his fingers into my panties, cupping my mound. One thick finger strokes my soaking folds, massaging my pulsing hole and gathering up my juices. He rubs my clit in excruciatingly slow circles, making me whimper and writhe at his touch.

"Fuck," he groans as he kisses his way down my body, trailing his lips and tongue over every dip and curve. His thumbs hook into my leggings and underwear, slowly sliding them down my body.

When my pants are half-way down my legs, Logan looks up at me, silently asking my permission. I bite my lip and nod, wiggling my hips to encourage him.

A feral sound leaves his throat as he tears my clothes off. I cry out in surprise, then moan when I feel his calloused hands skimming up my calves, knees, and thighs, coaxing me to spread my legs for him.

I gladly do.

Logan kisses a sensitive spot behind my knee and then nibbles on my inner thigh before moving to my other leg and doing the same. He finally gets to my center and I'm shaking with nerves and excitement.

"Relax, sweetheart. You're incredible. This pretty little pussy is soaked for me, isn't it?" I gasp when I feel his hot breath tease my soaking folds. "That's it, beautiful. I want you begging for my tongue."

He spreads my legs further apart and kisses the soft crease of skin where my legs meet my body. He runs his nose up and down both sides of my pussy, driving me crazy.

"P-please!"

Logan chuckles and I feel the sound vibrate through every part of me, down to my core. "Please, what, angel?" He uses his thumbs to spread my lips, still not touching me where I need him most.

"Please..."

He blows into my now exposed pussy, the warm air hitting my throbbing clit. The sensation overwhelms every part of me.

"Please lick me," I moan, already on edge from his teasing.

"Gladly," Logan growls.

His tongue dips into my entrance and roams up my slit till he gets to my clit. He sucks the nub into his mouth and I explode.

"Oh shit, oh shit..." I moan over and over.

Logan drinks up my honey like he's dying of thirst. He never lets up, bringing his thumb over my clit and massaging the sensitive nerves through my orgasm. He spears his tongue into my entrance, in and out, over and over, again and again.

He groans into my pussy, sending vibrations through my core and driving me right up to the edge again.

"God, Spencer. You're so fucking wet for me. I love having your cum on my tongue. Do you like me eating out your greedy pussy?"

"*Yes...*" I moan, my orgasm fighting its way to the surface.

He growls again and doubles his efforts, thrusting two fingers in my pussy while he sucks on my clit. I'm incoherent as I moan and thrash under his skilled fingers and tongue, grabbing his hair and pulling him closer to me, no longer able to keep my arms above my head.

I'm flooded with sensations, every nerve ending on fire. I feel myself gushing all over his hand and I can't bring myself to care. The tension builds in my core, my muscles tighten, preparing for the inevitable release.

He bites my clit and I lose it. I scream his name and come. *Hard.*

Logan licks me again, but I push him away, whimpering, too sensitized. He reluctantly pulls away, breathing heavily.

"I can't get enough of you," he growls, licking me one last time from bottom to top.

He crawls back up my shaking body, claiming my mouth in a soul-crushing kiss. I taste myself on him and it turns me on even more. Logan finally pulls away, both of us panting and sweating. He rolls onto his back and takes me with him, draping me over his body.

"Was that what you needed?" he asks after we've caught our breath.

I nod against his chest, molding myself to him. I don't think I could move if my life depended on it. Logan grunts as if confirming something. I smile against his chest, just picturing him writing that down on the list he's keeping on me.

"Thank you," I murmur, clinging to him.

The last thing I remember is Logan kissing the top of my head and whispering how beautiful I am before tucking the blanket around both of us. This is my new happy place.

# Chapter 9

*Logan*

Despite sleeping on the floor of a one-room cabin in the middle of nowhere, I had the most peaceful night of sleep in my life. All thanks to the sweet angel currently curled up on my chest.

The fire died hours ago, but the first rays of sunlight are peeking in through the window, lighting up the cabin with a soft orange glow.

Spencer mumbles something in her sleep, then turns her head and buries it into the side of my neck. I chuckle and skim my fingers up and down her spine as she snuggles closer. The weight of her body in my arms, her warm skin rubbing against mine, her soft breaths against my neck...it's perfect. She's perfect.

And for some reason, this goddess wants me.

She trusted me with her body last night, baring herself to me in a way I know she's never done before. Fuck if that didn't make me feel like a king as I peeled her clothes off and licked every inch of her curvy little body.

More than that, she trusted me with her fear. Spencer didn't say much except that she didn't like being in the dark, but her actions told me everything I needed to know. She woke up alone, in a dark room, in a strange place, and her first instinct was to find me.

My chest grows tight just thinking about it.

Waking up to her pressed against my side was the best feeling in the world. Second only to making her come on my tongue.

I swallow down a groan and will my dick to go down. I know it's a losing battle, however. It always is when Spencer is in the room, so how the hell can I control myself when she's naked and draped over my chest?

My phone rings, cutting through the early morning stillness.

Spencer makes the most adorably grumpy sound before snuggling deeper into the blankets. I grin at her as she steals the covers right off my body. I don't even mind. If it makes her happy, I'd buy all the blankets in the world and wrap her up in them every morning.

The phone rings again, and this time it's me who groans. I carefully readjust Spencer, who is somehow still fast asleep even as she clutches the blankets tightly around her. I can barely make out the freckles sprinkled over her cheeks and nose from beneath the cocoon she made for herself.

It takes everything in me to stand up and leave her there, but I know this call is important. Grabbing my phone, I throw a shirt on and a pair of shoes and make my way outside to answer the call.

"Logan," Marcus barks out over the phone.

"Marcus," I answer, running my free hand through my hair. He doesn't seem very happy with me. That's fine, because I'm not very happy with him, either. I did some digging last night and found some pertinent information Spencer's father left out about her stalker.

"Spencer is safe?"

"Yes," I confirm. At least he asked about her first. That wins him some points, but not enough to make up for his withholding information from me.

"Good, good," he says with a sigh, the relief evident in his voice. "Did you get anything on the fucker who tried to break in?"

"How do you know he was trying to break in?" I ask.

"Well, I assume he was. Why else would someone scale the wall and sneak into the backyard?"

"To leave a note like they have in the past?" I say pointedly. After a moment of silence, I continue. "Why didn't you tell me the notes Spencer got were left inside the property? It wasn't safe for her there."

"That's why I hired you. She's safe with you, and look, you got her out of harm's way."

I grind my teeth together and swallow back the growl stuck in my throat. "What aren't you telling me?" I grunt. I know what he's not telling me, but I want to see if he fesses up to it.

"I...It's not...Look, Logan. It's not what it seems."

"And what does it seem like?" I'm surprised he said anything at all, though Marcus still didn't confess to anything.

"You already know, don't you? Otherwise, you wouldn't be asking me these questions."

"Humor me."

A long, tension-filled moment stretches between us. I can hear Marcus's labored breaths as he decides what to tell me. He knows I know something, but he's not sure what or how much. That right there is almost as good as a confession.

"I've worked with him in the past," Marcus says softly.

"*Him* being Spencer's stalker? The person threatening her life and sneaking onto your property? Just to be clear," I spit out.

When I looked up the license plate number of the car from yesterday, I discovered it was a rental, which isn't surprising. What was interesting, however, was that the man who rented it is here on a visa all the way from beautiful Paris, France. I don't believe in coincidences, especially in my line of business.

"Yes," Marcus growls. He's pissed. Good. So am I. "That's none of your concern though, Logan. I hired you for your muscle, not your investigative skills."

"It's one and the same for me. In order to protect Spencer, I have to know what the threat is. Jesus, Marcus, why didn't you tell me?" I have to pull the phone away from my face to calm down a bit. I'm still missing a few pieces, and I know yelling at him isn't going to help.

"All that matters is that I'll be back soon. This latest stunt...it changes things."

"What? What things? What are you—"

"I'm handling it," Marcus snaps. "Just keep Spencer safe."

"Marcu—"

"I'll call later in the evening to check-in," he says, ending the call abruptly.

I gape at my phone, not sure what to do. *What the actual fuck?*

My hand squeezes around the shitty piece of plastic and glass, but I relax my hold, not wanting to snap the damn phone in half. I take a deep breath, and then another, willing my muscles to uncoil and my heart to calm the fuck down.

"Logan?"

All the anger drains out of me at the sound of her voice.

I turn to see my sweet, sleepy angel padding her way out onto the deck, all wrapped up in a blanket. My feet carry me toward her before my brain has a chance to catch up.

When I'm standing right in front of her, Spencer tilts her head back to look at me. God, her brown eyes are full of such wonder and awe. Is that look really directed at me? She smiles, making those golden flecks sparkle in her irises.

Game over.

I tangle my hands in her hair, holding her in place as my lips cover hers. Spencer gasps then moans so softly, so sweetly, I have to give her more. I have to give her everything.

I nibble on her lips, then lick inside her mouth, tasting her innocence mixed with her lust. Christ, this woman is going to kill me with how effortlessly sexy she is.

"More," she whispers, her words caressing my lips before I swallow them down.

Spencer drops the blanket and wraps her arms around my neck, pulling herself up. I growl in approval, my hands sliding down her naked body as I lift her up. She clings to me, her mouth never leaving mine as I walk us back inside the cabin.

I'll deal with Marcus later. Right now, I need to take care of my angel and give her everything she's asking for.

After shuffling my way inside, I untangle Spencer and set her on the ground, though I don't let her get very far. My hands slide up and down her curves while I kiss her soft, already swollen lips. She melts against me, her body becoming pliant as I kiss and touch and feel all of her, everything she is.

Spencer runs her hands up my torso and loops her arms around my neck, pulling me back down for a punishing kiss. I open up and take what she's offering, meeting each frantic stroke of her tongue with just as much passion and need as she's giving me.

She closes her eyes and tilts her head back, breaking our kiss so she can gulp down air. Her hands drift down to my biceps, where she grips me tightly, keeping me in place. I'm sure as fuck not going anywhere.

I can't keep my lips off her for one goddamn second. I kiss down her neck and lick the hollow of her throat before nipping the sensitive skin there. Spencer moans and digs her nails into my flesh, making me growl and grind my hard-as-fuck dick into her heat.

"What do you need, angel?" I murmur against her trembling flesh.

"Everything," she moans.

"You'll have to be more specific," I say as I kiss my way up her neck. My lips brush against the shell of her ear as one hand trails down her body until I'm cupping her pussy. "You want my tongue in here?" I rasp, circling the tip of my finger around her pulsing entrance.

"Yes," she gasps.

"How about my cock? Are you going to let me take your cherry, Spencer?"

Her eyes pop open, glowing with lust and hunger. Good.

"How did...?"

"How did I know you're an innocent little lamb?" Spencer nods, drawing my attention to the pulse pounding on the side of her neck. I graze my lips over the spot, then nip her flesh, growling when she shudders in my arms. "Because I'm the big bad wolf and I want to eat you whole."

"Logan," Spencer half moans, half whimpers. "Please...please do that. I want all of you. Don't make me wait."

Hearing her beg for me is sweeter than anything I've ever experienced. A wave of pleasure rushes down my spine, drawing my balls up tight and making precum leak out of me like a damn faucet. Fuck, this woman is my undoing.

She leans in at the same time I do, our lips crashing together as our need amplifies. Her desperate kiss mirrors my own, her eager hands clawing at me and begging me to give us what we both want. More.

I lift my woman up into my arms once more and head to the bedroom. Spencer deserves so much better for her first time, but I'll make it up to her. I don't know what the future holds, only that Spencer is the most important thing in my life from now on.

When we reach the bedroom, I toss her on the mattress and then strip down, adrenaline pumping in my veins and urging me to claim her right the fuck now.

Spencer is spread out for me on the bed, her silky auburn hair a tangled mess, her swollen lips slightly parted, and her chest heaving with shallow breaths. Goddamn, she's gorgeous.

I climb on the bed and crawl up her body, kissing her thighs, torso, breasts, neck, and finally, her sweet lips. I rub my body against hers, needing that friction, needing to feel her skin against mine.

"Logan, please, please..."

"Jesus," I grunt before claiming her lips. Spencer surprises me by sucking my tongue into her mouth, owning this kiss as much as she owns the rest of me.

It starts off slow, with tentative licks. I groan at her innocence but manage not to take control. Yet. Spencer explores my mouth, then pulls my bottom lip through her teeth, making me growl. She grins mischievously at me, and fuck, it physically pains me to hold back my orgasm. Shit, this can't be over before it even begins.

"You like knowing you have control over me, beautiful?"

"Mmhm," she nods, her lip twisting into a flirty smile.

Spencer gasps and then giggles as I flip our positions so she's on top. "Then take it, baby. Take control."

She braces herself on my chest, pushing herself up and adjusting to our new position. For a second, Spencer looks unsure of herself, but all of that vanishes when she sees my angry cock trapped between our bodies.

Spencer grabs the fucker and squeezes, *hard*. "Jesus Christ," I growl as I clench my fists. She grins again, knowing exactly the kind of power she has over me.

I slide my hands up her thighs and squeeze, helping her rock against me. My fingers glide over a faded scar running up the side of her right leg. It must be from one of the multiple surgeries she had as a girl. I massage her slightly raised skin, committing it to memory. I will always remember how lucky I am to have found Spencer. How lucky I am her life didn't end that day.

"I'm right here," she murmurs, her soft little hand covering mine.

"Damn right you are," I grunt, sweeping my eyes up and down her gorgeous body. She's here with me, and right now, my priority is to make her feel as much pleasure as her curvy body can handle.

Spencer licks her damn lips as she rolls her hips, rubbing her pussy up and down my shaft. The head of my cock taps her clit and she shivers, repeating the motion.

I reach out and cup her tits, weighing them in my hands and brushing my thumbs over her nipples.

"Yes," she hisses out, her movements stuttering as she leans into my touch.

I play with her hardened peaks, twisting them and plucking them while Spencer claws at my chest and rubs against me, getting herself off without me even entering her. Fuck, it's so damn hot watching her get all worked up, knowing I have so much more in store for her.

Spencer's movements grow frantic as she writhes on top of me. I feel her cream dripping from her pussy, so close to coming already. A shiver runs down her spine and she holds her breath, preparing for her orgasm. I feel it pushing forward, demanding to be felt, making her whimper with each breath.

Right before it takes her under, I grip her hips and hold her still. Spencer looks down at me with confusion and frustration, but then understanding dawns on her when I line myself up with her entrance. I groan when I feel her tight little channel pulse around the head of my cock. Goddamn, her greedy little pussy is trying to suck me inside.

"Ready for me, Spencer? Ready to be mine?" She nods, her deep brown eyes glossed over with lust as she circles her hips, trying to get me where she wants me. I hold her in place above me, not giving in just yet. "I need your words, angel. Tell me how much you want this."

"Logan," she whines. "I want to feel you inside me. I want to feel how we fit together. I want you to be my first and..." Spender trails off, looking away from me.

"First and what, Spencer?"

"First and last," she whispers, still not meeting my eyes.

"Look at me," I say gently but firmly. She lifts her gaze, those brown eyes capturing mine once more. "I want to be your first and last, Spencer. I want us— this—forever. You know that, right?"

"I..." Her voice trails off, but her eyes never leave mine. She gives me all of her doubts, her insecurities, her secret pain I've only just begun to understand. I take it all and silently promise her she's safe with me, always. "Forever," she whispers before slowly sliding down my cock.

"Fuck," I grit out, gripping her hips to help her take it slow. Her pussy is so damn *tight*.

"Logan," she breathes out, her entire body shaking when the tip of my shaft bumps up against her barrier. "Do it for me?"

I tip my head back and groan, biting the side of my cheek to keep from exploding in her creamy little cunt right this second.

"Yeah, baby. I've got you."

I lift her up slightly, then thrust up inside her, breaking through her virginity. I growl as I hit the end of her, grinding my teeth together to keep from flipping her over and rutting into her.

Spencer whimpers and I lean up to kiss her pain away. "You're perfect," I say, trying to make my voice soothing even though the most intense pressure is building up inside of me, ready to take over and fuck my woman properly. "Take it slow, we have forever."

She nods and kisses me again, her tense body relaxing ever so much as I run my hands up and down her thighs and back. I grip her ass and help her rock against me and circle her hips, finding what feels good.

"Yes!" Spencer cries out, wiggling her hips and hitting her G-spot against my thick dick. She shudders and moans, rolling her sexy fucking body on top of mine, totally taking control of her pleasure.

She leans back, resting her hands on my thighs and baring her beautiful body to me while she rides my cock. I slide one hand up her torso while the other squeezes her ass and opens her up even more for me.

I cup her breast and pinch her nipple, groaning when more of her cream spills out. Jesus, I barely manage to keep it together when I look down and see where we're connected. Watching her tight, wet little cunt stretch obscenely wide to take in my many inches is something I'll remember for the rest of my life.

"That's it, Spencer. That's so fucking it," I growl, moving both of my hands to her hips, jerking her up and down as I meet her thrust for thrust. Her pussy flutters around me as her muscles lock up tight.

Spencer falls forward, resting her hands on either side of my head. Her lips find mine, consuming me with her passion.

She buries her face into the side of my neck and sobs as her body shakes and tightens around me. My beautiful woman bites my neck and creams all over my cock as she reaches her climax.

Feeling her orgasm absolutely devastate her snaps something inside of me.

I roll over, changing our position and fucking into that little pussy, unable to control myself. Her back bows off the bed and her legs wrap around me, holding me close. She digs her heels into my ass and claws my back, leaving her mark on me as another orgasm rattles through her.

"So good, baby," I growl, before claiming her lips as my own.

I devour her, biting at her lips and spearing my tongue inside of her eager mouth, licking up every inch and then sucking on her tongue. It's a wild, messy kiss, one that matches the way I'm fucking her like a goddamn animal.

I slide one hand down her body and grip her ass cheek, changing the angle of her hips and helping her meet me thrust for thrust. My cock scrapes against her most sensitive spot with each fierce stroke.

I can feel her breaking apart for me. Every time I hit the end of her, she cracks a little more, the pressure of her orgasm building and pulsing and pushing her boundaries.

My balls draw up tight as my own orgasm gathers in the base of my spine. My rhythm falters slightly as I try to hold on, needing her to come with me. "Get there, baby, fuck, please get there. Need one more from you."

"It's too much, I can't..."

"I've got you, Spencer. Let go for me, I'm right here. Come for me."

She sucks in a huge breath and holds it, her whole body trembling and then freezing. Every damn muscle is pulled so tight as she clings to me with everything she has. With one last brutal thrust, we both shatter completely.

Spencer floods my cock with her release, and I give her everything in return, my cum splashing into her throbbing pussy as it sucks down every last drop. We're both grunting, shaking, and sweating as we ride that high together.

Eventually, she goes limp in my arms. I bury my face into the side of her neck and pump into her twice more before collapsing. I roll to the side and drape my freshly fucked little angel over my chest.

"Holy shit," she mumbles into my chest, her voice all scratchy as she catches her breath.

"Yeah," I agree, just as worn out and awed as she is. I mean...fuck. If I didn't know before, I definitely know now. She's it for me. "Are you okay?" Doubt and worry rush in to take the place of euphoria. "I was so rough with—"

Spencer cuts me off with a kiss. "You were perfect," she whispers into my lips before kissing me again. "Absolutely perfect. I can't wait to do it again."

I curse under my breath and tangle my fingers in her hair, angling her head to deepen our kiss. My cock is sore from how hard I fucked her, but damn if he isn't twitching to life, ready for another round.

Spencer moans softly, rubbing herself against my aching dick, apparently having the same insatiable thoughts I am.

"Angel," I groan, nuzzling into the side of her neck. "Need to feed you."

"I know what you can feed me..."

I roll her onto her back, caging her in with a hand on either side of her head. Spencer giggles, the joyful sound wrapping around every part of me and making me feel lighter and happier than I've ever been.

She smiles up at me, her golden-brown eyes full of laughter and glitter.

"I promise I'll feed you that later," I murmur, kissing her throat and grinding my cock against her thigh. "But right now you need real food. To keep your strength up."

She pouts, then laughs when I tickle her. I can't say I've ever tickled anyone, but her reaction lets me know she likes it. I'll add that to the list.

"No fair!" she gasps in between bouts of laughter.

"Yes, fair," I counter, stepping away from the bed before she can grab me. "Now get some clothes on and join me in the kitchen for breakfast."

Spencer pretends to be annoyed with my bossy tone, but her cute little smile gives her away. God, this woman is too precious for words.

# **Chapter 10**



"There you are," Logan greets me, walking over to pull me into his arms.

"Here I am," I say with a smile, getting up on my tiptoes to plant a kiss on those ridiculously delicious lips of his.

"You look so fucking sexy wearing my clothes," he says, his voice gravelly and dark.

I bite my bottom lip, then lick away the sting. Logan makes a tortured sound and I look up at him, giving him what I hope is a seductive smile. I opted to wear one of Logan's shirts, loving the way it hangs down to my thighs and smells perfectly like him.

I won't lie, I came out here in hopes for a repeat performance. My newly discovered libido is out of control, and I just knew wearing his shirt and no panties would send him over the edge.

As if reading my thoughts, Logan presses his hips into me, letting me feel his need as well. He backs me into a wall and licks the shell of my ear before nipping my earlobe. My breath catches in my throat and my pussy grinds down on his hard length.

"Gonna fuck you against this wall if you keep that up. Is that what you want?"

I nod as he sucks on my neck, groaning softly as he leaves little love bites on the tender skin there.

"Need your words, angel. Tell me what you want," he growls into my skin. I'm lost in the feel of his teeth, his tongue, the way he's devouring me. Logan's hand drops from my hip to my inner thigh. I part my legs for him as he skims his fingers up, up, up.

"Jesus, you're dripping for me," he groans, sliding a finger up my slit. "Say it, Spencer. Tell me what you want."

"I, oh God, I want..." My words are cut off by a long, keening moan. Logan presses one finger into my slick entrance, slowly thrusting in and out. "Fuck me, Logan. Hard," I moan.

"Whatever you say," he replies with a satisfied smirk. I love that look on him. I think I'm going to love what comes next even more.

I hook my thumbs into the waistband of the basketball shorts he has on and help him pull them down. His cock springs free and my hand automatically wraps around it. I feel his shaft throb in my hand, growing impossibly harder as I stroke up and down.

Logan grabs my hand and lifts it away. "I'm not gonna last if you do that. Need inside your perfect pussy."

He grabs my thighs and lifts me up. I wrap my arms around his neck and my legs around his hips. Logan thrusts into me in one swift motion, pushing all the air out of my lungs. I breathe him in, letting the smell of sweat and sex fill me up.

His dick hits the end of me with each stroke, tearing me apart in the best way possible. It hurts so good, his cock destroying me, both of us groaning, crying out, grunting our pleasure.

My muscles tighten, my pussy pulses, but I hold off my release. My entire body arches, my throbbing clit aches, but still I hold on. Desire, pleasure, and sweet pain push me into a new place. My world drips into a pinpoint of pure pleasure.

My orgasm hits me hard as Logan rams his cock deep inside. I bite down on his shoulder and he roars his release, bucking his hips into me to prolong our pleasure.

I open my eyes and realize I must have passed out for a second. My head is resting on Logan's shoulder, and his body vibrates as he chuckles.

"You okay, angel?"

I lift my head and smile up at him, still a little dazed. He places a chaste kiss on my lips and slowly pulls out of me, gently setting me back down on the floor. I lean into him, my legs still not working right.

Logan wraps me up in his arms, holding me close while we breathe together. "That was amazing," he murmurs, kissing the top of my head. "But I was going to feed you breakfast, remember?"

I tip my head up and smile at him. "Totally worth it." Logan gifts me with a rare smile before pressing his lips to mine.

"No more distractions," he says, stepping away from me. "I need my woman satisfied in every way."

After scrounging up what we could for breakfast, Logan went outside to chop some more wood for the fire. He's only been gone about thirty minutes, but I already miss him.

I've fallen head over heels for the man, that's for sure, and last night only solidified my feelings.

My cheeks heat up at the memory, even though it's just me and my art supplies in the cabin. It feels scandalous to think about the way his thickness stretched me wide open, the feel of his skin rubbing against mine, his unrelenting kisses...

I squeeze my thighs together, then take a deep breath. It's hardly been a few hours since I had sex for the first time, but I want more. So much more. I want to hear his ragged breathing in my ear as he thrusts in and out of me. I want to feel him come inside me again. I want to have his baby.

*Holy. Shit.*

Did I really just think that? What the hell is wrong with me? I mean, I know I'm obsessed with the man, but thinking about kids after knowing him for hardly more than a week is a whole new level of insanity.

It feels right, though. The thought of starting a new life with Logan, having a family with him, and finally finding a place where I can be both safe and free...it's so real, so raw, so overwhelming my chest aches. I rub the heel of my hand over my heart, trying to keep my emotions in check.

I don't want to be the cliché woman who becomes clingy after losing her virginity. It would kill me if Logan grew tired of my presence. So far, he seems as enamored with me as I am with him, but will he still be interested after a month? Six months? A year?

I try squashing down that thought, but it's a stubborn bastard. Years of watching my dad take off on business trips across the country and the world has left me with some insecurities. If my own father tries to leave every chance he gets, why would anyone else stick around for too long?

A crunching sound draws my attention back into the present. I freeze and hold my breath, trying to be completely silent as I listen for more.

*It's just Logan*, I tell myself. He's outside chopping wood and doing wilderness, mountain man things, whatever that entails. Plus, the cabin is in the middle of a dense forest, so there are lots of wild animals scampering about.

After a few moments of silence, I let out my breath and take a few more, willing the nagging feeling in the pit of my stomach to go away.

I focus my attention back on my current art project. It's going to be a mixed-media piece with a blend of traditional painting, magazine cutouts, found objects, and probably some glitter. I haven't decided yet, but I like to leave my options open when it comes to flair.

Right now, I'm just in the blocking out phase. I was struggling to find inspiration for so long in my art, but then Logan showed up and gave me lots of...*inspiration*.

I giggle to myself at my dirty thoughts, the smile lingering on my lips as I remember the heated moments we've shared as well as the tender ones. Logan is so sweet, though I think he reserves that just for me. I like that I can bring out his softer side.

Opening up my pencil case, I grab three different gradients of sketch pencils, then get busy laying the framework out on the canvas. The more I think about what I want to make, the more my mind wanders to Logan's sculpted body, the way he moved inside me, consumed me, broke me, and made me whole.

I want to capture what we shared.

Not just the passion and pleasure, but the very core feeling of being together like that. I want to somehow show him how much he means to me and how perfect we are together.

For someone who can talk a mile a minute whenever anyone is around to listen, I'm not always the most graceful with my words. My art, however, can convey emotions I didn't even know I had. I hope it can do the same for Logan.

Flipping through some of the magazines I packed, I find a few racy ads for women's perfume and men's underwear. I almost pass them up, but then my eye catches on the curve of the woman's shoulder and the cut jaw of the man in the underwear ad. The isolated lines and curves are almost more seductive and teasing than the whole picture. I cut both ads out, smiling to myself as I get lost in the creative process.

Over and over, I'm drawn to pictures of light and dark, sunshine and shadows, raging fire and pure white snow. The contrast speaks to me, something about the yin and yang of it all, the balance of the universe that I feel like I've only just begun to understand.

Logan may be jagged edges and darkness, and I may embody light, airy innocence, but we've been shaped by our pain. I still don't know Logan's whole story, but I don't need to. I've seen his heart, the way he treats me like I'm precious, and how he can't seem to believe I want to treat him the same way.

I don't know if my silly art project will mean as much to him as it does to me, but I have to try to communicate my feelings somehow. Logan's never made me feel silly about my art, though. In fact, he's only ever made me feel confident in myself and my passions, whether it's birds, art, or talking endlessly about nothing at all.

Something scrapes against the side of the cabin, causing me to jump and drop my scissors. They make a loud clattering sound on the table, but I hardly hear it over my pounding heart.

I don't think that was a wild animal. It sounded too...

The front porch creaks as someone walks up the steps. A whimper gets caught in my throat as tears burn the back of my eyes. I don't think Logan would use the front door if the woodshed is out back, but what do I know?

My wishful thinking dies the instant the front door splinters open.

I don't even think about what I'm doing until the scissors are flying through the air. It takes me a second to realize I threw them at the intruder. A wave of pride surges through me, but quickly dissipates when the scissors merely bounce off the man's chest and fall to the floor.

*Shit.*

Panic grips my heart, sinking its claws into old wounds while leaving fresh ones behind. My bravado slips as the man takes another step closer to me.

"Feisty, are we, *ma cherie?*"

My eyes snap up to meet the intruder's. I'm surprised that he has a heavy French accent, but I don't focus on that for long. Instead, I take in his tall, lean frame, dark eyes, and prominent nose. He looks familiar, but I don't know why. I don't recognize him, exactly, but he's not a complete stranger, either.

I'm sweating, shaking, and barely able to drag in a breath, but I tap into some hidden reserve of strength I didn't know I had. The scissors were the only thing within reaching distance that closely resembled a weapon, but I don't let that deter me.

I grab the first thing my hand touches, not risking taking my eyes off the man I'm safely assuming is my stalker. The magazine goes flying in the air, the corner of it hitting the side of the man's cheek.

I smirk as a thrill shoots up my spine. I grab another and another, hurtling them in his direction. Each one hits its target, but the man keeps advancing, his lips twisting up into a sinister smile.

"Your fight only makes me want you more, *cherie*," he says, his voice deep and dark. "I'm glad you didn't die alongside your mother."

"W-what?" I stammer out. "Who are you?" My fingers grope around the tabletop in search of my next weapon. Before he gets a chance to answer, I launch an open bottle of craft glue at him, hitting him in his ugly mug.

He makes a startled noise, then growls low in his throat. "Careful, Spencer. Turnabout is fair play."

The man starts wiping away the glue dripping down his face, but I don't back down. Paintbrushes go flying through the air, followed by an open container of pink glitter, a tube of navy blue oil paint, and more magazines.

"*Encule toi salaud*," he mutters. I don't speak French, but I assume he called me some not-so-nice words.

My stalker is now covered in glue, paint, glitter, paper, and who knows what else. I should run while he's distracted, but it appears I used up the last bit of my bravery. Now the panic comes back in full force.

"That's more like it, yes?" he says, his dark eyes glowing with satisfaction. "I like you better scared. Are you going to cry for me, *ma cherie*?"

Time slows as he reaches into his jacket and pulls out a gun. A pathetic sound is torn from my throat and my knees nearly give out. I can't die like this. And for what? I still don't know who this man is or why he's obsessed with me.

"Not so brave now, are we?" he taunts as he lifts the gun up higher so it's aimed right at my head.

I can't take my eyes off his trigger finger. For one brief, terrifying second, I think he's going to pull it and end my life right here in this remote cabin.

Instead, the gun slips out of his hand, which is still dripping with wet glue and paint. I watch the matte black metal object clatter to the floor and spin toward me. It takes my shocked brain a second to kick in, but I manage to bend down and grab the gun. I have no idea how to shoot the damn thing, but I feel better with it my hands, however shaky they may be.

"Now, now," he says, holding his messy hands up. I'd laugh at the site of my stalker covered in art supplies, but I hardly have enough air in my lungs to keep from passing out. His eyes are still hard and determined and his sick smile is back, but his voice betrays his nerves. "Why don't you—"

"No!" I shout, cutting him off. I don't have a plan here; I just know I somehow gained the upper hand and I can't risk losing it. "Get on your knees with your hands behind your head." I've heard that in cop shows before, so it seemed like the right thing to say.

"Funny, I was planning on asking you the same thing soon enough."

My stomach rolls at the implication of his words. Bile rises up in my throat at the thought of this man touching me, hurting me, forcing me to do unspeakable things.

He takes advantage of my shock and lunges for me, but he slips on the pile of magazines I was keeping at the foot of the table. The man smacks his head on the edge of the chair and shouts out in pain.

"Stay," I yell at him, training the gun on the man lying prone on the floor. I'm trembling so much my teeth chatter, but I don't dare move from my position. A sob wracks my body, but I swallow back the tears.

Just as I'm about to have a full-on panic attack, I hear the most comforting sound in the world. Logan's roar rips through the small cabin, his heavy footsteps coming closer and closer until he's standing in the kitchen, taking in the scene.

Our eyes lock and I know everything is going to be okay.

# Chapter 11

*Logan*

Spencer's wide, terrified eyes meet mine, spiking my already dangerous levels of rage and adrenaline.

It takes me a second to comprehend the scene in front of me. My angel is standing in the kitchen with a gun pointed at a man covered in glitter, paint, and a myriad of other shit. What the hell is going on?

It happens in an instant.

The momentary distraction I provided Spencer made the intruder brave. He sweeps his leg under Spencer's feet, causing her to fall backward and land with a thud. I lunge toward the man as the gun smacks against the ground, setting off a shot.

Spencer screams and the motherfucker tries reaching for the gun, but I grab his throat and pin him to the ground. With a knee on his chest and my hand squeezing his neck, I hold him in place while looking over my shoulder at Spencer.

She's sitting on the floor with her knees pulled up to her chest and her arms wrapped around her legs.

"Are you hurt?" I growl. I know my tone is harsh but I can't help it. This whole fucking thing is messed up and I'm bursting at the seams to beat this man into a bloody pulp.

She shakes her head no as a shiver runs through her body. I scan the room, looking for the gun. When I see it on the other side of the living room, I let out a breath of relief. The bullet hole in the front door puts me more at ease, knowing it didn't hit my angel.

"Go to the other room, Spencer. I'll take care of this." I squeeze the fucker's throat for emphasis, making him choke and sputter.

"No," she says, her voice trembling. I stare at her for a second, not sure I heard her right. "I'm not running away scared this time," she murmurs, her voice a little stronger than before.

As much as I want her to lock herself in the bedroom and hide in the closet until I've dealt with her stalker, I can't help but also be proud of my woman. I have no idea what the fuck just happened, and I'll never forgive myself for not being here, but Spencer was a fucking warrior today. She wants to see this all the way through to the end, and damn if I don't respect the hell out of that.

I nod once, then lift the sputtering man up by his throat and slam him back down on the floor, knocking the wind out of him. Then, I flip him on his stomach, grabbing his right arm and twisting it behind his back. The man screams out in pain as I increase the pressure, then drag him to his feet.

Holding him in front of me, I walk two steps to the nearest wall and shove his face into it while keeping him pinned down.

"There's a zip tie in my bag," I tell Spencer, nodding toward the duffle bag next to the couch. "Front pocket."

She stands up on shaky legs but holds her chin high as she makes her way to the couch. Goddamn, she's a vision. The image of her pushing through her fear, even though tears pour down her cheeks, will be burned into my memory for all time.

I grip the back of the man's neck and turn him roughly before shoving him to the ground. He grunts but doesn't fight me. He knows I'd crush his windpipe in an instant. Spencer is by my side a few seconds later, handing me the zip tie. I twist the intruder's arms behind his back, around one of the legs of the solid oak dining table, then secure his wrists.

Once he's subdued, I lean back and stare at his beady black eyes before surveying the damage. I smirk when I see a bump in his previously perfectly straight nose, blood pouring down his face from the break.

I cock my fist and punch him square in the jaw, pleased when he spits out blood and a tooth. The little shit whimpers, then glares at me.

"Fuck you," he chokes out.

I wind up to hit him again, but then I feel a soft hand on my shoulder. Spencer is still right next to me, her brown eyes focused solely on mine. I want to rip this fucker's throat out, but Spencer is silently telling me that's not the right thing to do.

It goes against every single one of my instincts to step away from the man, but I obey my queen. This is her moment, after all.

"Who are you?" she demands, crossing her arms over her chest. I take in my brave warrior goddess as she glares at her stalker. She's still pale and trembling slightly, but her jaw is set and her mind is made up. She's not going to let her fear rule her anymore.

"Claude Dubois," he sputters out.

"What do you want from me?"

His bloodied lips pull into a sickening grin. I'm about to slap the look off his face, but Spencer shocks the hell out of me by doing it herself.

"Bitch!"

I growl and take a step forward, clenching my fists at my sides. The urge to end his life courses through me, but I stand firm, letting Spencer continue.

She shakes her hand out, then grimaces when she sees the blood on her hand. She wipes it off and then crosses her arms once again. How is she so adorable and badass at the same time?

"My queen asked you a question, shit stain," I bark out.

"Yeah," Spencer says, shuffling closer to me. I pull her into my side, wrapping an arm around her waist to hold her steady. I know my girl is going to crash soon.

Claude hesitates for a moment, but then must realize he's fucked. He sighs defeatedly and hangs his head. "At first I wanted to finish the job," he mumbles.

"Speak up," Spencer practically yells at him. She's shaking from the adrenaline, every muscle in her body tight with tension. Yet here she is, staring her stalker in the face and demanding answers. I'm so damn proud of her.

"Fifteen years ago, you were in a car accident, yes?" My eyes go wide and Spencer straightens up, holding her breath. She nods once. "It was no accident, *ma cherie.*"

Spencer lunges at him, shocking the hell out of me once more. I loop my arm around her body and pull her into me, her back to my front. "Finish strong, love," I murmur into the shell of her ear. "Don't let him deter you."

"Explain, fuck head," Spencer shouts. I grin at my feisty, determined woman, tightening my hold on her.

"Your father took everything from me. He bought my family's company all those years ago. Stole it right out from under my feet as I was preparing to take over. I was groomed for that position since I was a boy, and then he ripped it all away. All I did was repay the favor by taking everything away from him."

"How did you…?" Spencer can't finish the question, but Claude doesn't need much encouragement to continue. He's in too deep now. It's almost like he's bragging about his plan, proud to finally tell someone of his actions.

"He stole my company but not my connections. It's incredibly easy to hire a hitman with the right amount of money and notoriety. It's even easier to fake accidental deaths. I thought both of you died in that accident, but I found out through a mutual business partner that you were alive and well." Claude licks his lips and drags his eyes up and down Spencer's body.

"Get your filthy eyes off of her," I growl, the sound more animal than human. "You're not worthy to be in this goddess's presence, let alone fucking look at her."

Claude glares at me and I narrow my eyes at him, a snarl falling from my lips. He darts his eyes away and clears his throat.

"I was going to finish the job like I said," he continues. "Hire another hit and take you out. But your father kept you locked away in that mansion. When I sent the hitman to do recon on you, he came back with pictures. I decided I didn't want you dead. I wanted you as mine."

"Those letters, the poem, the rose...that was you trying to woo me?" Spencer asks incredulously. "Never mind. Don't answer that."

I see the moment she realizes the other confession he made. Her chin quivers and tears well up in her eyes. She looks so broken, so damn vulnerable as she stares at the man who killed her mother.

And then she gets angry.

She digs down deep, tapping into the fire burning underneath the shock and grief.

"You can't hurt me anymore," Spencer says. Her voice is soft, firm, and unyielding.

My woman spins around in my arms and gets up on her tiptoes before crashing her lips on mine. My body responds immediately, opening up for her and letting her take her fill. My fingers tangle in her hair as I grip her tightly, angling her so I can deepen the kiss.

I can taste her strength and power on the tip of her tongue, and fuck, it turns me the hell on.

We're both breathing heavily by the time we break apart. "Did you say what you needed to say?" I whisper onto her lips. Spencer nods her head, rubbing her nose against mine. "I can take it from here. Go clean up and wait for me in the bedroom." Spencer nods again, then gives me one last chaste kiss before untangling herself from my embrace.

I wait until I hear the shower turn on, and then I crouch down in front of Claude. I let the repressed rage flood my system now that Spencer is safely out of the way.

"You're not the only one who can fake an accidental death," I seethe. Claude's eyes go wide and for the first time, I see genuine fear reflected in them. Good. I'm thankful I thought to call the contact

Colton gave me for the safe house. River, the president of Chaos MC, answered right away, assuring me he'd have three of his men there pronto. In fact, I hear the rumble of their bikes pull up into the gravel driveway.

I lean back and deliver a punch to his right eye and then to his stomach, making him cough up blood. I'm about to strike again, but then I hear feet shuffling on the porch before three men dressed in black jeans and leather jackets walk through the destroyed doorway of the cabin. I stand up and turn to face them.

"Logan?" the tallest one asks. I nod in confirmation. "I'm Jax. This is Dom and Carter. We're the backup from Chaos."

I try to speak to them in a normal voice, but I'm far too worked up for that. Instead I grunt and nod my head. Thankfully, it doesn't seem to faze Jax.

"You said you needed help taking out the trash?" His eyes drop to Claude, then rest on mine once more. I know he has a million questions about the man covered in paint, glitter, and now blood. He knows better than to ask them, however.

"This fucker thought he could kill my woman's family and then come for her without any consequences. He thought he could take her from me," I growl.

All three men get a fierce look in their eyes, as if they know something about fighting for the women they love. I know nothing about these men, but with one look, I know we're on the same page.

"Full cleanup, then?" Carter asks.

I nod once, knowing exactly what he's asking. I want this piece of shit wiped off the face of the earth, and I trust that these three know how to get the job done. I'd do it myself, but my woman needs me to comfort her, not get more blood on my hands.

"We'll take it from here," he assures me.

"One last thing," I say, turning to Claude. "How did you find us?"

The sick fuck smiles, even though he's living on borrowed time.

"I followed *ma cherie* home from her favorite craft store a few weeks ago. She set her bags down when she got inside the front gate to go fill up the bird feeders. I stuck trackers on as many of her things as I could before she came back for them."

I look over at the craft supplies surrounding the table, chairs, and floor. He could have killed her then and there, or at the very least, kidnapped her. But he bugged her instead. He's evil and predatory and I don't feel an ounce of remorse for erasing him from the face of the earth.

I focus my attention on the miserable fuck and kick him in the ribs before stepping out of the way. I wait on the far side of the kitchen, watching Jax and the other men cut the zip tie and haul a half-unconscious Claude out of the cabin.

A few minutes later, I hear three bikes pull away from the cabin, the sound of their powerful motorcycles trailing off down the driveway and onto the dirt road leading away from the cabin. I have to steady myself on the kitchen counter, the fight and adrenaline leaving my body all at once and making me lightheaded.

I take a deep breath and lift my hands from the counter, grimacing when I see the bloodied prints I left behind. I have to go check on Spencer, but she doesn't need to see me like this, nor does she deserve to clean up the kitchen after everything that went down today.

I try to gather my thoughts as I quickly but thoroughly scrub down the kitchen counter, the table, and the floor where Claude was sitting. Sifting through her art supplies, I find several dime-sized tracking devices stuck to the bottom of paint bottles and other random things. I peel them off and continue cleaning up.

Jesus, hearing Spencer shout and then a loud scuffle coming from inside the cabin was the worst moment of my life. I've never moved so fast. One second I was on the far side of the property, piling the wood into bundles to carry back inside, and the next I was bursting through the backdoor of the cabin.

After scrubbing away the last of the blood from the floor, I rinse off my hands and splash cold water on my face. I dig around in my bag and find a clean shirt, throwing it on after tossing the dirty one in the garbage can.

I take one last deep breath and then make my way to the bedroom. Spencer is standing by the window, freshly showered, with a soft smile on her lips. How is she still so soft and sweet after what just went down?

She turns to me, the late morning sun streaming through the window and silhouetting her frame. Big brown eyes look up at me, trust and strength shining through. Spencer's smile widens when she sees me, like I'm somehow completing her. I hope so, because she's become vital to my existence. I'm drawn to her like a magnet, and soon she's in my arms with her face buried into the side of my neck.

"What has you smiling, love?" I whisper.

"There was a chickadee outside," she whispers back. "They're my favorite bird."

"They make you happy?"

Spencer nods, then kisses the side of my neck. I hold her closer, needing more of her sweetness and light. "They are so small and precious. And they chirp a lot, kind of like me." I can feel her smiling against the heated skin of my throat.

I pull back slightly, just enough to cup her face in my hands. "You're small and precious. You make me happy. You're my chickadee." Tears well up in her eyes before spilling onto her cheeks, and I wipe them away with my thumbs.

"You're too good to me," she murmurs.

I press my lips to her hairline, breathing her in. "I'm not, but I want to spend the rest of my life trying to be everything you need. I want to earn your love, Spencer. It would be my greatest accomplishment."

She gasps and leans away from me, though I keep her close to me. "Love? You love me?"

"So goddamn much, chickadee." Her eyes go soft as a brilliant smile spreads across her face. I bend down and rub my nose against hers, letting the familiar gesture comfort and soothe my aching soul. "You filled in all the dark places in my heart without even trying," I whisper. "You're so beautiful, so talented, so fucking brave and sweet. I don't deserve you, but I need you. I'm keeping you, if you'll have me."

Spencer slides her hands up my chest and then grips my beard, pulling me impossibly closer. Her lips are an inch from mine. "I love you with everything in me, Logan," she murmurs. Her lips brush against mine as she declares her love for me. I steal the words right off her tongue in a claiming kiss.

My woman wraps her arms around me and pulls herself up my frame. Gripping her thighs, I lift her up, clinging to her as tightly as she's clinging to me. I walk us a few steps forward and then gently lay Spencer out on the bed before crawling in next to her.

She turns to face me, snuggling against my side. "I'm so proud of you," I tell her.

"You, too," she murmurs, resting her head over my heart. I can feel the weight of the day melt away as she relaxes against me.

"Get some rest now, love. I'll be right here."

# Chapter 12



*Spencer*

I wake up in a cold sweat, a scream caught in my throat as my heart thuds painfully in my chest.

"I'm right here, love," a voice says, cutting through the confusing panic in my mind. "You're safe. It was just a dream. You're safe now, chickadee."

Hearing the giant of a man soothingly call me chickadee snaps me back into the present. My nightmare still clings to my subconscious, the lingering fear making me tremble and whimper softly.

"I've got you," Logan murmurs, gathering me up in his arms.

I curl up into his chest, laying my head over his heart and letting the steady rhythm ground me. Logan skims his fingers up and down my back in calming strokes, the warmth of his skin seeping into mine and making me feel safe and loved.

After a few moments of silence, Logan leans down and nudges my head up. His striking blue eyes meet mine, such concern etched on his face. He rubs his nose against mine and hums soothingly, as if I'm calming him down, too.

"What's wrong?" I whisper.

Logan nuzzles into the side of my neck, placing a light kiss there. "I failed you," he murmurs, his voice full of emotion. "It was my job to protect you, and then when we met...it became so much more than a job. It was my priority, my purpose, my honor to provide you safety. And then this morning..." he trails off, his voice breaking at the end.

"Today you let me fight my own battles while supporting me the whole time. Even when you weren't there, I knew you'd come. I knew you'd save me."

"You saved yourself, my brave little chickadee."

I smile at his sweet words and kiss him on the forehead. Logan gives me a goofy little grin, then kisses me on the forehead as well before getting me settled on his chest once more. He combs his fingers through my hair and holds me close.

"You saved me, too," Logan says so quietly I almost don't hear him.

"What do you mean?"

He sighs heavily and doesn't say anything for a few moments. I have a feeling he's debating whether to tell me more or to brush it off. I pray he lets me in, lets me see that tender heart of his I know he's buried way down deep for so long. I want to provide safety for him, too. He can protect us from the dangers of the outside world, and I'll protect all the pieces of his soul that he gives me.

"My story isn't pretty, angel," Logan rasps out. I can tell he's struggling to stay strong for me, but he doesn't have to. I'll cover his weaknesses if only he'd let me.

I snuggle closer and run my fingers through his beard. I don't know why I love it so much, but Logan seems to like it, too. I'll have to start my own list of what makes him happy. Placing a kiss over his heart, I hope to silently convey I'm here and ready to listen.

"I grew up in a trailer park in a shitty Philadelphia neighborhood. I was mostly raised by the other parents in our section of the park since mine were too strung out to remember they had a son most of the time."

Tears spring into my eyes as my man opens up and bleeds for me. I know how much it's costing him to tell me all of this.

"I've only ever seen the kind of love that hurts. The toxic kind that suffocates you and traps you in a prison of hate and bitterness. My parents fought all the time. Sometimes they got violent, but mostly they screamed and threw things around until they either passed out from exhaustion or got another fix."

"I can't imagine growing up like that," I whisper, tears pouring freely from my eyes. "You deserved better from them."

Logan squeezes me and kisses the top of my head. "I ran away when I was seventeen," he murmurs, the sound muffled by my hair. "I got into some trouble out on the streets. Mostly stealing luxury cars and flipping them. I found myself in the middle of a turf war one night after jacking a car. It took nearly catching a bullet in the chest to shake me up and realize I was going to die young if I kept up that lifestyle."

"What did you do?"

"Joined the military. That's how I know your father."

"My dad!" I gasp, starting to sit up. Logan pulls me back down and wraps his arms around me, keeping me pressed against his chest.

"Don't worry about him," Logan says in his deep, calming voice. "I called him after you fell asleep this morning."

"You did?" Logan nods in confirmation. "What did he say? Wait, what did you tell him? About Claude or..." I can't finish the thought. Did he tell my dad we're together?

"I told him the threat has been eliminated. I also said he should have taken better care of you," he mutters. "More importantly, though, I told him I found the woman I want to spend the rest of my life with. I told him I was going to make you my wife as soon as you agree to it."

I sit up and this time Logan lets me. My mouth is hanging open as I stare at him. Logan has a soft smile on his lips, one I've only recently seen him give me. I can see doubt linger in those beautiful blue eyes of his, though. This man is giving me his heart, his past, and now his future. Who could say no to that?

I lean forward and rub my nose against his. "You didn't really ask," I say with a grin.

"Marry me," Logan demands, making me giggle.

"That's telling, not asking," I laugh. Logan nips at my bottom lip, pulling it through his teeth before claiming my mouth.

His tongue tangles with mine, each stroke growing more frantic until we're both clawing at each other. By the time we break apart, we're both panting.

"Maybe I should *show* you some of the benefits of being my wife," he growls softly.

"Yes, please." The words are barely out of my mouth before he seals his lips over mine. The kiss is devastating in its intensity, and I swear I feel it in every part of my body.

Logan tears himself away from me and pushes himself off the bed. He practically rips his clothes off, then rids me of the oversized shirt of his I was wearing.

I only have a pair of panties on underneath, and Logan makes some sort of deep groaning sound in the back of his throat as I stretch out on the bed and let him get his fill. I may not have had much contact with the outside world, but I know I have more curves than most people. Logan loves my body, though. I can feel it whenever he touches me, even if it's innocent. He craves me as much as I crave him.

"Need to taste that pussy before I fuck it," he growls, fisting his cock and pumping up and down. I stare at his thickness, my thighs clenching and my clit throbbing at the memory of having him inside me.

Logan kneels down by the edge of the bed and grips my ankles, tugging me so my ass is almost hanging off the bed. I squeal and he nips at my thighs, causing me to giggle and then moan when he licks away the sting. Logan slips one leg over his shoulder and then the other. I'm spread wide before him with just a thin scrap of lacy panties separating my pussy from his face.

"Jesus, Spencer..." Logan presses his nose into my panties and breathes me in. I feel his thumb rub me through the thin layer of fabric, melting away my heartbreak and turning it into pleasure.

"Yes," I moan breathily as he works me over. I'm already on edge and he's hardly even touched me.

With an animalistic grunt, Logan rips my panties off and dips his tongue inside my pulsing channel, dragging my juices up, up, up until he's circling my clit.

"So damn good," he says more to himself than to me.

Logan dives back in, licking sucking, and devouring every inch of my pussy. I feel his tongue, his teeth, his hot breath working in tandem to wind me up tighter and tighter. He shoves two fingers deep inside of me and curls them up. My back arches off the bed and I scream his name, riding the sweet edge of torture and pleasure, ready to fall into oblivion at any moment.

He continues to thrust his fingers in and out of me as I writhe and buck my hips. "Yes! Yes! Ohmygod, I'm...I'm..."

"That's it, love, come for me. Come so damn hard, Spencer."

He leans in and sucks my clit into his mouth, pushing me over the edge. I grind against his face as my legs tremble and snap around his head. Every muscle spasms and I can't breathe yet as wave after wave of pure ecstasy floods my veins, threatening to suffocate me. I don't mind. I don't ever want to come up for air. Logan laps up everything I give him, growling into my folds and holding me closer so he doesn't miss a drop.

I'm vaguely aware of Logan pulling away and scooting me up the bed, but my mind is still in a fog of pleasure as I come down from that high. My pussy is still swollen and throbbing when Logan thrusts his huge cock inside of me.

We both cry out and my legs hook around his hips, my heels digging into his ass and pulling him closer.

He slowly pulls out and then kisses me at the same time he shoves his hard shaft back into my depths. My cries are swallowed down by an all-consuming kiss as he sets a steady pace.

Logan breaks the kiss only to trail his lips down my throat and collarbone until he flicks his tongue over one aching nipple and then the other. He licks and nibbles and sucks the tender flesh of my breasts until I'm writhing beneath him. I meet him thrust for thrust until his pace turns frantic.

"Fuck, angel, just...fuck."

He slides his hand between our bodies and rubs my clit. Over and over, he rolls the little bundle of nerves in between his fingers. I close my eyes as my muscles tense and lock up, preparing for another orgasm.

"Logan! Don't stop, please, don't—"

And then he's not touching me. He's not inside of me. He's not even on the bed.

"What...?" I pant. I'm a needy, horny mess and I need his dick to fix it.

I feel his hands on my hips. Logan flips me over and smacks my butt cheek, chuckling.

"I'm not ready for this to end yet. Up on your hands and knees, baby. Show me that ass."

I do as he says. I feel his hands grabbing and massaging my ass, appreciating all of my curves. Then he leans over so his front is covering my back and nibbles the shell of my ear. "I've got you, chickadee. I'll always give you what you need."

With that, he slams into me from behind and I come on the spot. Hard. I hear someone scream out in pleasure. Some part of me knows I'm the one who made that sound, but it feels so distant. I feel so far away, like I'm on another planet looking down on us as Logan fucks me good and hard.

"Holy fucking shit, baby, that's it. Squeeze my big dick."

My whole body pulses around his cock as he pistons in and out of me. One orgasm rolls right into another, my juices running down my thighs.

"Lo...gan...so...good!" I say in between thrusts.

He grabs my hair in his hand and twists my head so he can bend down and kiss me. I get lost in the way our lips melt, the sound of our skin slapping together, the feeling of our sweat mingling and dripping down our bodies.

When we come up for air, Logan grabs my hips and ruts into me like an animal. I push back into him and he growls, the vibrations spreading through his cock and straight into my pussy. He massages my ass cheeks and pulls them apart.

"Jesus, fuck, baby. Love watching us like this. My cock stretching your pussy lips...goddamn. Love watching you take all of me like a good girl. Are you a good girl, Spencer?"

"Ye...Yes!"

"Are you going to come for me again?"

"Mmhm..."

Logan slows his pace a little and spanks me. It sends a jolt of white-hot pleasure to my clit.

"Words, baby, I need your words. Are you going to come for me?"

I try to pull in enough air to form words, but I can only manage to nod my head yes. His other hand comes down to spank me on my other cheek.

I moan as the sting intensifies all the pleasure I'm already feeling.

"Mmmore..." I moan.

"Shit..." he groans.

He picks up his speed again and smacks my ass once, twice, three times. I explode right as his hand makes contact the fourth time.

"Fuck, Logan, ohmygod..."

"Jesus, Spencer..."

He grips my hips tight enough to bruise and he stills inside of me. I feel his cock swell up as my pussy massages him over and over. He roars his release as it shoots out of him and paints my insides. I hope we create a life today. I want that so bad it hurts.

We're both breathing heavily as Logan pulls out and crashes down next to me. He rolls me over and throws me across his chest so he can hold me. I rest my head over his heart and listen as it slowly returns to a normal beat.

I look up at him and he has his eyes closed. He's rubbing small circles on my naked skin, sending shivers down my spine.

Finally, he cracks one eye open and looks down at me. His face breaks out in the most adorable grin. God, could this man be any more perfect?

"So, what do you say? Will you be my wife?" I smile at him, tears stinging my eyes. "Chickadee, why are you crying?" His face turns from joyous to concerned in an instant.

"They're happy tears." I sniffle, leaning in to rest my forehead on his.

"Would marrying me make you happy?" he whispers.

"Very much so," I say with a nod, brushing my nose against his. "You make me happy, Logan. You're at the top of my list."

He nuzzles into the side of my neck, kissing me there. I swear I feel tears wet my skin. "You're at the top of my list, too, chickadee."

We stay wrapped up in each other's arms, soaking in the love and happiness we somehow found in this crazy world.

Epilogue 1

*Logan*

"I can't believe you talked me into this," Spencer whispers.

I wrap my arm around her waist and tuck her into my side. She melts against me, letting me soothe her anxiety. I knew today was going to be a lot for my chickadee, but I'm so damn proud of her.

"I've watched you slay bigger dragons than this art show," I murmur into the shell of her ear before kissing her temple.

Spencer looks up at me and gives me a little smirk that sends my heart racing. She's somehow more beautiful than when I first met her eight years ago.

"Yeah, and there was plenty of paint and glitter that time as well." Her beautiful brown eyes sparkle up at me and I have to kiss her.

Leaning down, I rub my nose against hers in a familiar gesture of comfort. Spencer's lips pull into a smile against mine right before I claim her. She sighs so sweetly for me, parting her lips so I can drink from her and get my fill.

Someone clears their throat from behind me, breaking the moment. Spencer buries her head into my chest while I chuckle and squeeze her before turning to face the gallery director.

"You two are sickeningly sweet and all that, but we've got some very eager patrons waiting for the star artist to make an appearance." Ginny, the tall, slender woman Spencer has been working with to organize her showing, gives us a hint of a smile before her face turns serious once more.

Spencer takes a deep breath and straightens her shoulders. I give her hand one last squeeze before sending her off to meet her fans. As I watch her walk down the hall and into the main gallery, I have to blink away tears.

I'm a six-and-a-half foot tall, tatted-up motherfucker in a tux, standing in the backroom of an art gallery trying not to cry. Never in a million years did I picture my life turning out this way, but I couldn't be happier.

The last time I was in a tux was at our wedding. I cried then, too. I can't help it. My chickadee opened up all the dark places I kept locked up and made it safe for me to feel things again. Or, rather, feel things for the first time. Things like love, belonging, and peace.

I wait a few moments before heading out to the gallery myself. I want Spencer to fly tonight. Fuck that, I want her to soar, and I want her to know she did this all on her own. She filled canvas after canvas with her beautiful, untamed soul. And now she's showing her art to the world.

My eyes immediately find Spencer in her royal blue gown that hugs her curves and flows all the way down to the ground. Her auburn hair is pinned up, showing off her slender neck. My mouth waters just thinking about sinking my teeth into her creamy skin and then licking away the sting.

But dammit, I need to behave myself. I already showed her how much I love her dress when she bought it. I plan on doing the same when we get home tonight. Lucky for me, our daughter is staying at a friend's house tonight, so I can have my way with my sexy wife all damn night.

Spencer shakes hands with an older couple who are raving about one of her paintings. My chickadee blushes slightly but accepts their compliments and tells them more about the piece.

I know she's anxious, but I'm so proud of her for taking this huge step in her career. After we got married, I encouraged Spencer to switch her major to art studies and take classes in person. She cried, which devastated me until she said they were happy tears. I still don't like her crying, but I do like making her happy.

I like to think I've done a pretty good job of keeping my chickadee happy all these years. I still don't deserve her pure light and soft sweetness after the shit I've seen and done, but little by little, Spencer is showing me I'm worthy of her and worthy of our happily ever after.

Serena, our seven year old, is bright and bubbly just like her mother. She also has an affinity for messy craft projects. Good thing I love cleaning up after my girls and hanging up their art all over our house.

My favorite art piece from Spencer is the one she was working on the day she took her power back. I thought she would want to throw it away and rid herself of any reminder of that horrifying experience.

My queen was having none of that.

She finished it the next day. Spencer sat at that table for hours, crying as she painted and glued and bled all over the canvas. I was powerless to fix her pain, so I stood by and watched over her while she worked through the complicated emotions of learning the details about her mother's death. She also had to come to terms with her father's involvement, even if it was just withholding that information from her.

The two of them have patched things up over the years, though it's still tense when he comes to visit. Marcus was shaken to his core when I called and told him what Claude tried to do. He admitted he had his suspicions about his wife's death, which I already figured. Marcus knew his daughter's life was in danger, but it must not have sunk in just how much until it was nearly too late.

He was so thankful that I was there he almost didn't care that I staked my claim on Spencer. After the initial shock wore off, however, my military buddy had plenty to say about an old, ugly motherfucker marrying his only daughter. Too bad neither Spencer nor I cared about his opinion. When it became clear I wasn't going anywhere and that I would always protect Spencer, he came around.

It wasn't until little Serena came along that things started to heal between the three of us. Life is too fucking precious to hold onto grudges. At least that's what Spencer said. Who am I to disagree with my brilliant, beautiful chickadee?

"What are you thinking about?" Spencer's soft voice cuts into my reverie.

I turn toward her, smiling when I see those brown eyes with golden flecks. "You, of course," I say with a smile. Spencer cuddles up into my side and I wrap my arm around her before kissing the top of her head. "Are you happy with our life?"

Spencer leans back a bit, then tangles her fingers in my beard, tugging me down so we're face to face. She kisses the tip of my nose then nuzzles against me. "You make me the happiest woman in the world," she whispers. "You give me the confidence to spread my wings while also providing me with a safe place to land. How could I not be happy?"

"Just checking," I murmur, giving her a chaste kiss. Spencer tugs me down once more, sealing her lips over mine.

"You always make me happy," she says once we break apart.

I skim my fingers up and down her back and brush my lips against the shell of her ear. "And I always will, chickadee. I always will."

Epilogue 2

*Spencer*

"Mommy, Mommy, Mommy, wake up!"

I pop one eye open, looking at my beautiful girl. Sophie, our youngest, turned five last month, and she's such a little ray of sunshine. Her bright blue eyes sparkle as she gives me a toothy smile.

"Morning, sweetheart. What's—"

Sophie tugs at my arm before I can finish my thought. "Come *on*!" she urges, making me laugh. I throw on a robe and my slippers and follow her out into the kitchen.

"Happy anniversary, mom!" Serena says at the same time as Sophie. Serena, now fourteen, has a too-large apron tied around her with food spills all over it.

"What's going on?" I ask, looking around the disaster area that is my kitchen.

"You were supposed to go to the dining room so you didn't see the aftermath," Logan says from behind me, wrapping his arms around my waist and kissing my temple. "You look beautiful today, angel."

I know I look like a mess, but I truly believe he thinks I'm beautiful no matter what. My tummy flips every time he calls me angel. Even after fifteen years of marriage, my husband still has the ability to make me melt with a single word.

Logan guides me to the dining room, chuckling when Sophie and Serena dart ahead of him to sit at the table.

"Oh my gosh, what is all this?" I gasp, looking around at the feast spread out on the table.

"Ham and cheese quiche, fresh fruit and granola yogurt parfait, coffee, juice, and bacon for good measure," Serena says with a proud smile.

"Did you make this all on your own?" I ask her.

"I helped!" Sophie interjects, hopping up and down.

"Yeah, helped make a mess," Serena teases. Sophie sticks her tongue out at her sister and then bursts into giggles as Serena tickles her.

"Alright, girls. Breakfast time," Logan says with a chuckle. He pulls out my chair for me, helping me get settled. These sweet little gestures do me in every time. I'm reminded every day how lucky I am to keep this man for the rest of my life.

"Thank you, everyone. This is such a lovely way to start the day." I squeeze Sophie's hand and then Serena's, trying not to cry.

I try not to let a single day go by without being thankful for my family. For so many years, I was lonely and locked up. Then my Logan came and set me free. He's given me confidence in myself and has brought some much-needed structure to my chaos. He's also given me a precious family and continues to amaze me by how well he takes care of us.

Logan cups the side of my face, tilting my head up to meet his gaze. "Happy anniversary, love," he murmurs before bending down and taking my lips in a soft kiss.

"Ew!" Sophia squeals.

Logan chuckles, the deep sound vibrating through me. He gives me one last kiss and takes his seat next to me.

The four of us laugh and talk about the day ahead as we devour the delicious breakfast. Afterword, the kids dash off to their rooms to get ready for the day. I start clearing up the dishes, but Logan stops me with a hand on the small of my back.

"I'll take care of cleaning up. I have another surprise for you," he murmurs, kissing the side of my neck. I bite my bottom lip and look at him over my shoulder. Logan groans and presses a chaste kiss on my lips. "How is everything you do the sexiest goddamn thing?"

Before I can answer, my big, burly husband scoops me up in his arms and carries me to our room. I giggle and wrap my arms around his neck, kissing his chin. Logan closes the door with his foot and sets me down, pressing me against the wall.

The heat and hunger in his eyes sends a shiver down my spine, but it's the love and adoration underneath that warms me up. He's always looking at me like that, and it never gets old.

Dipping his head down, Logan trails his lips up my neck, kissing and nipping at my pulse point. "As much as I want to fuck you right up against this wall, I don't want to scar our children for life."

I huff out a laugh, then moan as he grinds his thick cock into my stomach. Logan threads his fingers through my hair, tipping my head up and crashing his mouth down on mine. I immediately open up for him, sliding my tongue against his and getting lost in his kiss. One after another, he bombards me with kisses, each one rougher, needier than the last.

I'm a panting, whimpering mess by the time he finally pulls away.

Logan rests his forehead on mine breathing me in. "Damn, woman," he whispers. "I'll never get enough of you. He surprises me by wrapping me up in his arms and rocking me back and forth. This man. He's equal parts sexy, insatiable beast, and sweet, caring protector.

"You said there was another surprise?" I ask once he steps away. Logan grins at me and goes to the closet, digging around for something. When he returns, he's holding a large picture frame.

I give he a questioning look, and my husband actually blushes. Now I *have* to know what's inside the frame.

"After fifteen years of marriage, I finally got the courage to make some art of my own," he says, giving me a little smile. "A beautiful chickadee once told me all about collages, so I thought I'd try my hand at one."

I'm speechless, tears already forming in my eyes as he turns the frame around to reveal a stunning collage. Gasping, I step forward and trace my fingers over the glass. He has photos of our wedding day, our girls, and the guys at Watchdog as well as their families. Logan also cut out photos of birds from magazines, along with beautiful, brightly colored flowers.

There are some darker colors and clippings in the bottom left-hand corner, including a car, a thick forest, and a gun. The images and colors get brighter and move vivid the further up the panting goes. Near the top, there's a healthy dose of glitter, which makes me sniffle and smile.

It's our entire history, even the hard parts. Dark, light, deep sadness, and unimaginable joy. I see it all in his display of love and vulnerability.

"So...? It's certainly not quality of artwork my talented artist of a wife is used to, but I hope you know it's genuine."

The tears fall freely down my cheeks as I nod, looking up into his sparkling blue eyes. Logan's face falls, but I'm quick to ease his worry. "Happy tears," I choke out, wiping my eyes. "It's beautiful. Perfect. I can't believe...just, thank you, husband."

Logan sets the frame aside and pulls me into his arms. "Love hearing you call me that," he whispers. "Love being your husband."

"I love being your wife," I murmur, kissing his chest right over his heart.

Logan nuzzles into the top of my head, making me smile at his sweet gesture. "I can't imagine my life without you, angel. You've given me more than I ever could have hoped for," he says with all the tender conviction in the world.

I soak up all of his love, letting it fill me up. This man has given me more than he could ever know. A life full of joy and laughter, a shoulder to cry on, a family we're both crazy in love with. He's shown me every single day that I'm worthy of a happily ever after, and I hope I give him the same.

Overcome with gratitude, I tilt my head up and kiss him slowly, deeply, before whispering, "Life without you doesn't exist. Let's stay married for another hundred years or so." Logan gives me a heart-stopping smile, rubbing his nose up and down mine.

"Would that make you happy?" he murmurs.

"Being with you forever is the happiest ending I could ever dream of."

"I'll make sure to move that one to the top of the list," he says with a playful smile.

I grin and snuggle closer, loving the way Logan hums with satisfaction as he tightens his hold. This right here? This is my happy place.

"Mine too, chickadee. Mine too."

# THE END

# Also by Cameron Hart

**Check out my other popular series and books!**
Mafia, MC, & Bodyguard Romance:
<u>Moscatelli Crime Family Series</u>[1]
<u>Di Salvo Crime Family Series</u>[2]
<u>Chaos MC series</u>[3]
<u>Savage Ride</u>[4]
Mountain Man Romance:
<u>Men of Blackthorne Mountain Series</u>[5]
<u>Bear's Tooth Mountain Men Series</u>[6]
Cowboy & Small Town Romance:
<u>Roped in by Love Series</u>[7]

---

1. https://books2read.com/u/mqBaze

2. https://books2read.com/u/m0odzW

3. https://books2read.com/u/bMVAOk

4. https://books2read.com/u/bMVlG7

5. https://books2read.com/u/3RYDvB

6. https://books2read.com/u/mVel7A

7. https://books2read.com/u/3RYlBY

www.ingramcontent.com/pod-product-compliance
Lightning Source LLC
Chambersburg PA
CBHW031425130726
47989CB00003B/1037